BEY

MELISSA TOPPEN

beyond love lies deceit

MELISSA TOPPEN

MELISSA TOPPEN

BEYOND LOVE LIES DECEIT

Beyond Love Lies Deceit

A Novel

Written by Melissa Toppen

MELISSA TOPPEN

TABLE OF CONTENTS

CHAPTER ONE
CHAPTER TWO
CHAPTER THREE
CHAPTER FOUR
CHAPTER FIVE
CHAPTER SIX
CHAPTER SEVEN
CHAPTER EIGHT
CHAPTER NINE
CHAPTER TEN
CHAPTER ELEVEN
CHAPTER TWELVE
CHAPTER THIRTEEN
CHAPTER FOURTEEN
CHAPTER FIFTEEN
CHAPTER SIXTEEN
CHAPTER SEVENTEEN
CHAPTER EIGHTEEN
CHAPTER NINETEEN
CHAPTER TWENTY
CHAPTER TWENTY-ONE
CHAPTER TWENTY-TWO
CHAPTER TWENTY-THREE
CHAPTER TWENTY-FOUR
CHAPTER TWENTY-FIVE
CHAPTER TWENTY-SIX
CHAPTER TWENTY-SEVEN
CHAPTER TWENTY-EIGHT
CHAPTER TWENTY-NINE
CHAPTER THIRTY
CHAPTER THIRTY-ONE
CHAPTER THIRTY-TWO
CHAPTER THIRTY-THREE
CHAPTER THIRTY-FOUR
CHAPTER THIRTY-FIVE

MELISSA TOPPEN

Chapter One

Samantha

The lobby of Sco-Tech is a sterile one. Clean lines, glass and steel make up the large area giving it a very expensive and futuristic feel. I guess I should expect no less from the nation's leading technology firm, famous for its motto; *We Are the Future.*

I shift in my seat, straightening the black pencil skirt I chose to wear for my interview today. It took nearly every penny I had to afford it, along with the cream colored silk blouse I'm wearing, but I knew a company like this would accept nothing less and I didn't want to take any chances where this job's concerned.

Not that I'm that worried. To be honest, I know they would be foolish not to hire me. I have a four year degree, a successful internship under my belt and some stellar references. If anything, I am over qualified for the position of Assistant to CFO Luke Scott, but it's not about the position, it's about the *in* it will give me into Sco-Tech.

I won't mention to them that my entire resume is falsified; that I am actually nineteen instead of the twenty-two year old that I claim to be, that everything about who I say I am is a lie. That I paid my neighbor to pose as my internship boss or that my name along with my social security number and college degree actually belong to a young woman that passed away in a car accident two years ago.

I have perfected it all. Each and every aspect of my identity and my past is sealed, a distant memory of a girl long since gone. Samantha Cole no longer exists, at least as far as the rest of the world is concerned anyways.

Taking a deep breath, I let it out slowly, trying to keep my nerves at bay. I've planned this, obsessed over it. I know exactly what I need to say, how I need to act. This is the final piece to assembling a puzzle I started laying out two years ago; to destroy those who have destroyed me.

Revenge is not the answer. There is no peace in vengeance. These are the things my mother taught me as a child. I must learn to forgive and through that forgiveness, will find the means to let go. To understand the present, you must first learn of the past.

I wasn't always this jaded broken girl, hell bent on destroying the lives of others. I was once an innocent. A young girl growing up in the suburbs of Boise, Idaho, I had a fairly simple life. My dad worked in sales and my mom taught second grade at the local elementary school. We didn't have a lot, but we had enough that we never wanted for anything.

My older brother Sean was the scholar of the family. Graduating from high school with honors, he earned a full scholarship to NYU. Sean was born to achieve great things. A star athlete and all around fun guy, there was not a person on this earth that met Sean who didn't love him instantly.

I was his biggest fan.

Being eight years older than me, my big brother was

my idol, my protector, the one person that I knew would always be there for me, until he wasn't. At eleven years old I had never even considered a world without Sean. But just three semesters after he left for college, a life without him was exactly what I faced.

The police said he was killed instantly, that he didn't suffer. That didn't make me feel any better. I would lie in bed at night and envision the pain that must have coursed through him when the car he was riding in lost control, flipping six times before finally coming to a stop. I imagined the fear he must have felt knowing that in one split second his entire life was over.

Ryan Scott, the driver, and Sean's fraternity brother, walked away with a couple of broken bones and minor lacerations but nothing life threatening. Ryan was the one driving after he had been drinking and yet he walked away while my brother paid the ultimate price.

A few weeks after the accident Ryan was charged with first degree vehicular homicide and faced some pretty serious jail time. At least he did, until a judge paid off by his father ruled that evidence of intoxication should be excluded from trial because he claimed law enforcement did not comply with procedures established for collecting the evidence. Ryan's sentence was reduced to vehicular manslaughter and he got off with a fine and two years' probation.

Equipped with more money than they know what to do with, the Scott family thinks they rule the world and the world has done nothing to show them differently. I guess operating Sco-Tech, a top firm for developing and selling computer software applications used by nearly every major retailer across the country, buys you a free pass where justice is concerned. And while Ryan and his rich father walked away and never looked back, Sean's death set into motion a series of events that can never be undone.

First was my mother. Overcome with grief, she lost her ability to function as a normal person. She self-medicated on prescription pain pills and anything else she could get her hands on. I found her dead of an overdose two years after Sean died. I was thirteen.

Next was my father. He tried to stay strong for as long as he could but the loss of my mother only further intensified his drinking and before long I was the parent and he was the child. It was less than four years after my mom's death that my dad would follow; massive heart attack at the age of forty-four.

That was it, I was alone. Every single person in my family was gone and there I was, seventeen and angry at the world. I had to find something to sink my anger into and I became fixated on the one thing that seemed to make me feel better; revenge. I am determined to make Ryan pay the way he should have paid eight years ago and take Nicholas down right along with him.

I know my family is probably looking down at me right now begging me not to do this, but it's already too late. I have sat by for far too long and watched my life fall apart because of Ryan Scott, while he carried on with his privileged happy life without a care in the world. No more.

He will pay...

"Miss Reynolds." I look up to see a petite woman in her mid-thirties standing over me, a curious look covering her pretty face.

"Yes." I stumble out, realizing she must have said my name at least once before.

"You can come with me." She gives me an

understanding smile, clearly chalking up my reaction to nerves. *If only she knew.*

"Thank you." I answer politely, standing.

She leads me down a long corridor to a set of double doors before turning left and leading me down another hallway. Finally coming to a stop at yet another reception area, she informs the older red headed woman behind the desk that I am Mr. Scott's eleven o'clock interview. The woman barely looks in my direction before picking up the phone and immediately informing whoever answers on the other end of the line that I am here.

"You may head on in Miss Reynolds." She informs me, hanging up the phone as she gestures to the massive set of double wood doors just to the right of the desk.

Nodding, I spin on my heel and quickly push my way inside, my eyes temporarily impaired by the dimness of the room in contrast to how bright the rest of the building is. There is a wall of windows that line the back of the large square space but they are shaded by some sort of tint, blocking out the natural light that would otherwise be flowing in. Even in the dim lighting, it doesn't take long for my eyes to land on the man sitting behind an enormous mahogany desk towards the back of the room; Luke Scott.

Luke Scott is the youngest son of Nicholas Scott and brother to Ryan. Of the two Scott brothers, Luke is a bit of a mystery. While I researched the family extensively, I found very little on Luke. From what I can tell, he seems to avoid the spotlight while his brother basks in it.

Working for Luke seems like the better route. It gives me the ability to acquaint myself with Ryan and

Nicholas without being in the lion's den, so to speak. Even though the ultimate goal is to get close to Ryan, I know I need to ease my way in. Though how I am going to do that I still haven't quite figured out yet.

Crossing the space towards Luke, my heart is beating so loudly, I swear he must be able to hear it pounding against my ribcage. The noise floods my ears and instantly makes my stomach twist. Knowing what needs to be done is one thing, actually following through with it is quite another. And while I have done everything in my power to ensure that all will check out, I am still terrified that somehow someone will discover who I really am, as if just looking at me will give it away.

"Miss Reynolds." Luke's deep voice fills the space just as I reach the chairs sitting opposite the desk, my eyes landing on his face.

I can't control my reaction as I take a deep sharp inhale the moment a pair of crystal blue eyes find mine and hold me completely captive. He stands, reaching out his hand across the desk.

"Luke Scott." He introduces himself, his smooth voice once again filling my ears.

I don't realize I have even moved until the warmth of his hand is suddenly surrounding mine. "Allie Reynolds." I manage to get out.

"It's nice to meet you Miss Reynolds." He gives me a warm smile causing my knees to shake slightly in spite of myself.

I've seen pictures of the Scott brothers before. Both Luke and Ryan are very attractive men but seeing Luke in the flesh is an entirely different experience. He has the kind of looks that stop you dead in your tracks. His features are strong, chiseled, as if he'd been etched from stone instead of being made of flesh and bone. His dark hair is short and perfectly styled, pushed away from his face, putting the beauty of his eyes on full display.

Draped in a black custom fitted suit, his six foot frame and muscular build seems massive next to my five two, one hundred and ten pound body. I feel suddenly very intimidated by his presence, or maybe it's his beauty that I find so unsettling.

I guess he must be used to this type of response from women; the sudden pause in her natural expression when she looks his way followed by a weak smile. Of course the blush that immediately follows my reaction is a dead giveaway of where my thoughts currently lie.

"Please have a seat." He gives me a knowing grin, gesturing to the chair behind me.

Nodding, I quickly comply, settling down onto the stiff leather.

"Get it together Sam. He's a Scott." I remind myself when he meets my gaze once more.

Straightening my shoulders, I push my hair away from my face, tucking the long dark blonde layers behind my ears.

"Thank you so much for coming in so quickly. This position opened up rather unexpectedly." He continues, shuffling through a stack of papers on the desk in front of him.

"Of course." I keep my reply short and professional.

"So, Miss Reynolds." Luke finally locates my resume, setting it directly in front of him on the desk. "Why don't we start off by you telling me a little about your internship with Advanced Global?" He meets my gaze again.

I quickly respond, spouting off one of my rehearsed answers about all the tasks I performed and experience I gained working as the assistant to Gail Osborne, VP of Sales for Advanced Global; a prominent marketing firm in the Los Angeles area.

"Well according to this letter of reference she was very sad to see you go." Luke chimes in the moment I finish. "Is there a reason you didn't stay on for a more permanent position? By the looks of it you definitely could have." He gives me a smooth smile causing my stomach to clench slightly.

"I enjoyed my time with Ms. Osborne immensely but overall the company wasn't the right fit. I want to work for a company I can grow and expand with. Unfortunately, marketing is not the field I want to pursue and while I gained a great deal of experience working for Advanced Global, I knew going in that my time with them would be a stepping stone, a learning experience to better assist me with where I ultimately want to end up."

"And is Sco-Tech somewhere you want to end up?" He asks, looking up from my resume.

"More than you know." I answer truthfully.

Whether it's for the reasons he's assuming is irrelevant. The statement stands true regardless.

"What is your ultimate goal in a career? I'm guessing based on your education that you don't want to be an assistant forever." His gaze on me does not falter.

I feel squeamish under the intensity of his eyes but I manage to keep myself together.

"I would love to be a financial analyst which is why I think this position is perfect for me. I feel like working as an assistant to the Chief Financial Officer will give me invaluable insight into what it takes to operate a multi-billion dollar corporation." I beef up my answer, hoping to come across as driven and eager to grow within the company even though not one part of my response holds any truth.

"Why Sco-Tech?" He asks a question I knew was coming.

"It's simple." I meet his gaze. "Sco-Tech has revolutionized the technology industry. It controls so much of a major market that working for any other company seems meager in comparison. Sco-Tech is the mother ship Mr. Scott, but then again I'm pretty sure you already knew that." I can't help but smile when he lets out a light laugh.

"I have got to hand it to you Miss Reynolds; you've done your research."

I'm not sure but if I had to guess I would say he views this as a good thing, though I could be wrong. Maybe he views it as me being too eager to impress which could potentially reflect negatively on me. Most people want straight shooting hard workers, not ass kissing know-it-alls. I hope I don't come across as the latter.

"It says here you graduated with your bachelor's degree in less than three years." He gives me an approving nod when I meet his gaze.

"Yes. I attended classes year round in order to cut down on the length of time I had to spend on my education." I confirm, nervously tucking my hair behind my ears again even though it has barely moved since the last time I did it.

Again, I'm not sure if he is impressed or annoyed with my response. Coming into this interview I felt like I had this in the bag but sitting in front of a man like Luke Scott has completely derailed my confidence and is causing me to second guess every word that leaves my mouth.

As Luke continues, I do my best to keep my answers straight and to seem unaffected by how much he wants to know. I must have practiced the answers to every question he asks a hundred times over but I still feel the heavy weight of doubt creeping in with each one I give.

Even still, by the end of the interview I am fairly certain that I at least have a shot. Besides being initially distracted by how attractive he is, I feel like I handled myself relatively well.

Standing, Luke once again extends his hand to me. "It was very nice to meet you Miss Reynolds."

"You as well, Mr. Scott." I reply, taking his hand, flinching slightly as his fingers tighten around mine.

Not that it's painful, not even close. It's more about the way his hand around mine causes my stomach to clench and my heart to pick up speed, even if just a fraction.

Pulling my hand away, I nod and smile politely before quickly excusing myself from Luke's office, eager to escape the confines of the four walls that I've felt closing in on me more and more as the time has passed.

As I exit the building just a few short minutes later, I can't seem to shake Luke's eyes from my mind. The way they studied me with each word I spoke, the way they seemed to burn traces into my flesh as he took in my appearance, the way they seemed to momentarily blind me from my very purpose for being in his office.

I find the whole thing unsettling and yet oddly electrifying at the same time. While I may be here for a very specific purpose, that doesn't mean I am any less human or any less of a woman. I would have to be blind not to be physically attracted to Luke Scott.

After walking for twenty minutes in less than comfortable heels, I finally reach my apartment complex, which sits a few blocks from Sco-Tech's Corporate Headquarters. I get two steps into the entrance of my building when my phone springs to life in my purse.

The sudden screeching causes me to jump slightly. Having just bought this phone two weeks ago, a cheap pre-paid phone I got at a nearby store, I am not used to having a cell phone. I know that sounds unheard of to most people but for me it just made sense. Why have a phone when there's no one alive that cares to talk to you?

"Hello." I say, holding the small device to my ear.

"Miss Reynolds." Luke's voice washes over me.

To say I am surprised that he is calling me personally, especially this soon after leaving his office, is a bit of an understatement. I assumed when I heard back about the position it would be from his secretary or someone maybe in Human Resources and not for at least a couple of days.

"Mr. Scott." I reply, trying to keep the surprise from my voice.

"I'm sorry to do this to you considering you just left a few moments ago, but I was hoping you could come back to the office sometime this afternoon." He says.

"Sure. Is everything okay?" I ask, praying the question doesn't seem suspicious.

"Everything is fine, great actually. I wanted you to come back to fill out your new employment paperwork." He replies casually.

"Employment paperwork… You mean..." I pause for a moment trying to calm my excitement. "I got the job?"

"You got the job." He confirms. "That is, if you still want it." There's a note of uncertainty in his voice.

"Of course I do." Again I try to keep the excitement to a minimum, afraid to come across too eager.

"If we can get you back in today for paperwork, we can get you started as early as Monday." He says, once again surprising me, given that it's already Thursday.

"Absolutely." I answer immediately.

After confirming all the details about meeting with Human Resources today at three o'clock, I hang up the phone, feeling a sense of satisfaction I have not felt in a very long time. Finally, after years of hell, Ryan Scott is going to get exactly what he deserves, and what's better, he doesn't have any idea it's even coming.

Chapter Two

Luke

"Word on the street is you finally replaced Katherine." My brother Ryan pulls my attention from the spreadsheet in front of me and I look up just as he flops down in one of the chairs across from my desk.

"I did." I confirm, looking back down at my laptop screen.

"Well don't act too excited Luke." He sighs, running his hand through is short sandy blonde hair while hitting me with an annoyed look.

"Excited?" I can't keep the sarcasm from my voice. "Why would I be excited about the fact that I had to give up my assistant because you can't keep it in your pants?"

"What are you talking about?" He tries to play innocent.

"Do not play stupid with me Ryan, Dad already told me what happened with Carly." I can't hide my irritation with my older brother.

"Jealously does not look good on you Luke." He gives me an arrogant smile, already knowing full well that jealously has nothing to do with the current issue I have with him.

"I'm not jealous. You and I both know I could have had her if I wanted. Unlike you, I have a moral code." I give him a knowing look.

My brother has always tried to make me feel inferior to him in every way possible. And while he tries to insinuate that he is the better looking of the two of us, we both know we look too much alike for him to make that claim. Other than the fact that I am about two inches taller and have darker hair than he does, you would almost think we were twins; at least when it comes to our appearance, personality wise we couldn't be more different.

"Give me a break." He sighs loudly. "Besides, Carly made her own bed."

"You mean she made yours, after you slept with her."

Ryan has always been what you would call a playboy. He goes through women quicker than anyone I have ever met and shows very little remorse over the trail of broken hearts he leaves behind him. Why women still get involved with him is beyond me, it's not like he tries to hide who he is.

Ryan's latest conquest left my father's assistant of three years out of a job and resulted in mine being transferred to my father's office to take her place. Considering Katherine is in her early fifties and has been with the company for over thirteen years, I guess my father felt like she was a safe bet to fill Carly's sudden departure.

"So tell me about this new girl." He raises his eyebrows up and down at me suggestively, wasting no time redirecting the topic of conversation.

"You're unreal." I shake my head in irritation. "Tell me again why Dad is prepping you to take over as CEO, because for the life of me I can't understand it?"

"Again with the jealousy Luke." His arrogance infuriates me but I manage to bite my tongue. "Chief Financial Officer is not a bad gig. Besides, we both know you're not cut throat enough to take on Dad's role." He gives me a look that dares me to challenge him.

"You mean I actually have a heart. Not going to argue with you there brother." I turn my attention back to the spreadsheet on my laptop. "Now if you don't mind, I have actual work that needs to be finished. You can see yourself out."

Pushing out of the chair, he mumbles something under his breath before swiftly exiting my office, clearly not happy with my reluctance to indulge in his little games.

Ryan is one of those people you hate to love. He's crude and arrogant, selfish, and dishonest, and it's very rare that he shows any emotion in regard to anyone but himself. Sure, he's fun to be around if what you're looking for is fun. But find yourself in a bad situation with him and rest assured that he will leave you high and dry without so much as a backwards glance. Something he has done to me over and over again, especially when we were kids.

You would think at twenty-eight, he would have grown up a little. Honestly, I think age has had the opposite effect on him. Even though he is two years older than me, most just assume that I am the older sibling.

Don't get me wrong, Ryan has some redeeming qualities. While I give him a hard time about his unprofessionalism in regard to the women we work with, when it comes to the actual company there is not a person that knows this business better than Ryan. Thanks in large part to my father who has spent the last ten years grooming his oldest son to take over his empire.

I try to put on a poker face most days where Ryan and my father are concerned but losing Katherine has left a bitter taste in my mouth. Katherine has been my assistant since I took over as CFO four years ago. She is very much like a mother to me. It guts me that she is going to have to work directly for Ryan one day. She's optimistic about the move and seems to be in good spirits, though I feel like a part of that is probably for my benefit.

It's not that I am not excited about Miss Reynolds, but I loathe such dramatic change. Even still, I am trying my best to take it in stride. She is very qualified and I'm confident she will be a good fit here. On the negative, she is also very attractive and young which means her success will hinge on whether or not I can keep her away from Ryan.

I let out a loud sigh, pushing my chair backwards away from the desk slightly to stretch out my legs a bit. This has been such a long day and unfortunately, I am also looking at a very long night. Being the person that oversees finances for a company operated by Nicholas Scott is no easy task. Especially right now with him being caught up in acquiring smaller tech companies and pulling them under the Sco-Tech brand.

There is a lot that goes into purchasing these businesses and my father rarely plans ahead with these acquisitions, which usually leaves me working all night to draw out the financials and contracts for a deal he wants to close in the matter of days.

Chapter Three

Samantha

"What do you say baby girl? Should we give it another go?" Sean smiles, standing over me from my place on the sidewalk, his hand extended out to me.

I look at his hand and then to the bike laying on the ground next to me. Do I want to try again? The pain in my knee tells me no but the encouraging look on Sean's face makes me want to say yes.

"You can't give up after one fall." He wraps his large hand around mine and pulls me from the ground.

Standing my bike next to me, he urges me to climb back on.

I hesitantly throw my leg over the frame, terrified of falling again but even more terrified of disappointing Sean. Taking a deep breath, I give him a weak nod before he begins pushing the bike, jogging next to me until he feels like I have my balance before letting me go.

The front tire sways and fear paralyzes me for a moment but I manage to recover and keep the handlebars steady. I peddle as fast as my legs will allow, riding all the way to the stop sign at the end of our street before realizing I made it. I actually did it.

Managing to stop the bike without wrecking, I jump off the seat and let the pink and purple glitter bike fall to the sidewalk. I turn towards Sean as he's jogging to me, an enormous smile on his face.

"I did it!" I squeal, jumping up and down as the realization sets in. "I did it!"

"You did it." Sean confirms, pulling me into his side in a one armed hug. "I told you Sam, you can do anything. You just have to be brave enough to try."

I shoot up in bed, my breath coming in quick pants as I try to shake off the dream, or rather the memory. Pulling my knees to my chest, I rest my head against them. I remember that day like it was yesterday. I was six years old and had been begging Mom and Dad to let me ride my bike without training wheels.

Being an impatient child, I couldn't wait for that weekend when they would have time to teach me. So after talking about it all morning, Sean finally agreed that he would teach me that day after school. He really was an incredible big brother.

We had our differences of course, what siblings don't? But those differences never defined us. Sean didn't just teach me how to ride a bike. Among many other things, he also taught me about something that after he died became an outlet for me; art.

Sean loved to paint. I remember sitting in the doorway of his bedroom watching him glide his brush against the canvas. He would work on one piece for hours and of course, wanting to be just like him, I had to learn how to paint too. Little did I know then, painting would be one of the only things to hold me together when everything else was falling apart around me.

Glancing at the half painted canvas in the corner of the room, a calm settles over me as I take in the colorful brush strokes and wild patterns that seem to depict the very way I feel most days; lost and without meaning.

It's been so long since I have dreamt of Sean. After having nightmares for months after I found my mom...

I stop mid-thought and immediately try to push it away.

I can't let myself go there. Not today. It must be the timing; the circumstances surrounding my life right now that is forcing the memories to come flooding back into my subconscious.

Shaking my head, I try to refocus. Today is my first day at Sco-Tech; the day I finally set my plan into motion. Throwing back my thick comforter, I look around my studio apartment. The tiny space consists of nothing more than a small kitchen, an even smaller living space, and a makeshift bedroom that all exist inside the same four walls. The only additional room is a bathroom so little that it is barely big enough to move in once you close the door. It isn't much and the part of town that I am in is less than desirable, but it was the only thing I could afford with the small amount of money I brought with me after my dad's life insurance had been processed.

It wasn't much but it was enough to get me from Boise to Los Angeles and to lease this apartment for six months. Standing, I cross the square space to my kitchen, which takes up the entire back wall of the room, before grabbing a bottle of water from the refrigerator. The walls inside the apartment are bare. The entire space is void of anything that would make it personal, containing only the items that are necessary for my survival.

My stomach twists as the reality of today washes over me. I don't know if I am more nervous or excited about my first day as Luke Scott's Assistant. I certainly did not expect the salary agreement I was offered upon hire. I will be making more than enough money to see me through until my plan is complete. Given what the position pays, I just hope I can do the job without raising too many red flags with my level of experience. Truth is I don't know the first thing about being someone's assistant.

I've done my fair share of research and am fairly confident I can fake my way through it, but like most things, there is an air of doubt that surrounds me and every single decision I have made since moving to Los Angeles three months ago.

"How is your first day going?" I hear Luke's voice causing me to immediately look up.

He's standing casually in the doorway of my small office that sits directly next to his, his hands tucked inside the pockets of his gray suit pants.

"It's going really well." I answer, giving him a polite smile.

"Did Katherine get you everything you need?" He asks, referring to his current assistant who is responsible for teaching me the ropes over the next week before she moves into her new position working directly for Nicholas Scott.

"Yes. I am just working on logging all of your meetings into the online calendar she set up for me. I should have it finished later this afternoon and be able to sync it directly with you later today."

"No rush." He pushes away from the doorframe and crosses the twelve by ten square foot office space, sliding into one of the two chairs that sit adjacent to my desk.

"I was hoping you could spare a few minutes to have lunch with me." He says, leaning back into the chair, crossing his arms in front of himself. "Think of it as a welcome to the company."

"Well, I… I have a lot of stuff to work on, first day and all." I immediately start to make excuses.

I wasn't prepared for the offer and finding a valid excuse when put on the spot proves to be rather difficult.

"Nonsense." He swipes his hand through the air. "Besides, I know the boss. I think he can spare you for an hour." He smiles, eliminating any ability I have to deny his request.

"Grab your purse, we can walk down together." He stands, hovering just feet from my desk until I have gathered my things.

Running my hands along my black slacks, I try to smooth out the material before following him out of the office. I can't stop my eyes from immediately landing on Luke's broad shoulders, completely fixated on how they move with each step he takes in front of me. There is something so powerful about the way he walks, so commanding. Honestly, I can't say that I have ever encountered a man quite like Luke before. Then again, my experience with men is somewhat limited.

Over the years it has become more and more difficult for me to form any type of real connection to another person. Not that I haven't tried. I even dated a couple of times in high school but nothing ever felt right and I found myself ending things before they ever really took off. The handful of men I have slept with were all just my pathetic attempt to make myself feel something, anything, but even that didn't take.

"Do you like Chinese?" Luke interrupts my thoughts, stopping to allow me to exit through the revolving door of the lobby first before following me out into the sunny March air.

"I do." I answer, sliding on my black pea coat jacket as a cool breeze whips around us.

"There's this incredible little place just a couple of blocks from here. It's one of Los Angeles best kept secrets." He grins, keeping a slow pace as too not make me struggle to keep up with him as he leads me down the sidewalk.

"Well you found it so how well kept could it be?" I respond, hoping my playfulness is not misconstrued as unprofessional. I am in such unfamiliar territory right now.

"Touché Miss Reynolds." He smiles playfully, his eyes giving off an almost twinkle in the sunlight as he looks down at me.

I can't deny that my heart picks up speed or that an explosion of butterflies erupts in the pit of my stomach with that one look but I do my best to seem as unaffected as possible. He clearly has a knack with women and I refuse to allow myself to be pulled in by someone like a Scott. I know too much about his family to look at him as anything other than the monster I'm sure he is behind the mask.

It takes us less than five minutes to reach the small restaurant tucked in between a flower shop and clothing boutique along a busy shop-filled street. Holding the door open, Luke waits until I enter before stepping in behind me.

"This way." He says, his hand falling to the small of my back as he leads me through the restaurant and into a small private room in the back that is blocked off by a swinging door.

I step inside, unsure as to why we would be eating back here and not out front with the other patrons, but my thoughts quickly turn the moment the small room comes into view and I spot the other occupants of the space. Sitting at a private table in the middle of the room just feet from where I am standing is none other than Ryan and Nicholas Scott.

My heart immediately kicks into overdrive, the sound of my own pulse so intense, I swear I can hear each and every beat. My breath comes in short spurts and my entire body seems to lock up. Before I can react, Nicholas has stood from the table and is crossing the space towards me.

Stocky and standing just around five ten, Nicholas Scott is not a huge man but like his youngest son, there is something so commanding about the way he walks. He carries himself with such confidence. His dark blonde hair is kept short and is peppered with streaks of silver around his temples.

It's clear to see the similarities between him and his sons but as I look between him and Ryan, who steps up next to his father, I can see the greatest resemblance is between the two of them. Luke has dark hair and is taller than the other two, and while Ryan clearly works out, Luke is a bit more built than his older brother as well.

"Miss Reynolds. It's so nice to meet you." Nicholas says, taking my hand and shaking it firmly the moment he reaches me. "I'm Nicholas Scott, founder and CEO of Sco-Tech." He says, clearly having no idea that I already know exactly who he is.

"It's very nice to meet you." I manage to get out, my voice sounding more like a stranger than the one I am accustomed to hearing.

Everything feels skewed and off kilter. And as I look to Ryan whose eyes immediately meet mine, it takes everything I have to maintain my composure. I have waited for this moment for years, obsessed over it actually, and now that it's actually here I find myself unable to react fully.

"Miss Reynolds, this is my eldest son Ryan, and the person training to become CEO of Sco-Tech." Nicholas gestures to the son standing next to him.

"Ryan, it's a pleasure." I say, feeling the cold seethe through my veins as our hands embrace on a shake.

Oddly, I find that the hatred I feel for this man fuels the barrier I need to maintain and a calm settles over me.

"And you Miss Reynolds." He gives me a flirty smile and I return it with one of my own. Two can play this game.

"Shall we sit?" Luke speaks, reminding me of his

presence.

"Let's." Nicholas answers, gesturing to the square four person table the two men were occupying prior to our arrival.

Following Ryan, I wait until he pulls out a chair and gestures for me to sit before taking my seat. Of course, he wastes no time settling in next to me and as Luke takes the seat across from his brother, it's not hard to pick up on his annoyance.

So Luke has a problem with how Ryan is with women. Something I am sure I can use to my advantage. Being here with the entire Scott family, having them so close to me, solidifies my place in the here and now. I am more determined than ever to see my plan through.

"So Miss Reynolds, Luke tells me you graduated from Stanford. I'm a Stanford man myself." Nicholas boasts, nodding to the young Chinese woman as she sets four waters on the table.

"I know. I have done a lot of research on Sco-Tech and its founder." I give him a nod and a smile.

"Well, you can't believe everything you hear." He laughs, pinning his brown eyes directly on mine.

"All good things." I falsely reassure him.

"Well in that case, believe away." He gives me another wide smile.

"Enough about him, tell us about you." Ryan pulls my attention to where he is sitting directly next to me.

"Not much to tell." I answer lightly.

"Now why do I not believe that?" He gives me a crooked smile.

I immediately notice that like his father, Ryan also

has brown eyes. I can't help but wonder where Luke gets those brilliant blue ones that look like they could cut through darkness. And while Ryan is almost as good looking in person as Luke, there is something about Luke that just sets him apart from the other Scott men.

I open my mouth to respond but then immediately close it when the waitress reappears to take our orders. Realizing I haven't even glanced at the menu, I quickly look over it making sure that by the time she reaches me, I know exactly what I want.

"So Miss Reynolds." Nicholas picks up as soon as the waitress walks away.

"Please, call me Allie." I insist.

"Allie." He smiles, nodding before continuing. "How is your first day at Sco-Tech going? Are you learning a lot?" He asks.

"Very much, thank you." Though I purposely do not tell him that what I am really interested in learning has nothing to do with the company but with his family, specifically his oldest son.

While I was not thrilled to find myself in a room with all three Scott men with absolutely no warning, I am now realizing that this is an opportunity I did not expect to have. My goal is to get close to Ryan and this is the perfect setting for me to set that plan in motion.

Turning my head to the side, I throw Ryan another flirty smile when I catch him looking directly at me. Not enough to show I'm interested but just enough to make him think that maybe I am. Enough that he will chase me just to prove to himself, and maybe even to his brother, that he can conquer me.

If there is anything I have learned about this man through my research it's that he has one fatal weakness; women. I intend to exploit that weakness and use it to unravel his perfect little life…

Chapter Four

Luke

There's something about this girl, something I can't quite put my finger on. On the outside she seems so fragile; beautiful and frail. Despite her big chocolate eyes and the way she twirls her hair around her finger so innocently when she's clearly nervous, there is strength to her, a power I can sense but can't seem to justify.

One thing is for sure, she sure knows how to handle my brother. I don't know if I should be disgusted or impressed by this fact. He has spent the entire lunch relentlessly trying to impress her and while her sweet smiles have not been in short supply, I can tell it's all an act.

A woman that is *not* interested in my brother?

I didn't know one of those existed, and yet she seems completely unphased by his attempts to charm her. Though I am not entirely sure he sees it, I can. I've watched too many woman fall at his feet not to miss one who is completely unaffected. And as Ryan turns the conversation once again in an attempt to keep her interested, I find it difficult to stifle the smile that slowly spreads across my face.

"What do you mean you've never been to Little Tokyo?" Ryan acts playfully appalled by this revelation. "I must take you there for dinner one night. They have the best sushi restaurant you can find in L.A."

"I'm actually not a fan of sushi." She admits, her petite shoulders rising in a small shrug while Ryan looks at her with wide eyes, as if he can't fathom that a person would not like sushi.

"How can you not like sushi?" He shakes his head in disbelief.

"Is it that hard to believe that someone would not like raw fish and seaweed?" She answers, clearly confused by Ryan's reaction.

"Actually, yes." He laughs.

"Alright stop hounding the poor girl over her choice in food." My father finally steps in, clearly growing tired of Ryan's need to hold Allie's attention completely to himself. "We really should be getting back." He says, pinning his eyes on my brother before turning to Allie. "Miss Reynolds, it was a pleasure meeting you. I hope you like it at Sco-Tech and don't hesitate to come to me if you ever need anything."

"I appreciate that." She smiles politely and then turns towards me, a small blush taking over her pale cheeks when she realizes I am watching her. Not wanting to make her feel uncomfortable, I quickly look away, turning my attention to my father as he stands from the table.

"How long until the Neilson account is ready to close?" He turns his attention to me as he slides his suit jacket on.

"I should have everything drawn up and finalized

this afternoon." I confirm, trying to focus on my father and not on whatever Ryan seems to be saying to Allie as he crouches down next to her, his voice hushed.

"Good man." My father says, pulling my gaze back to him just as he extends his hand to me. Giving it a quick shake, I turn my gaze back to my brother just as he straightens into a stand, my father stepping up next to him. "Ryan lets go." He says.

My brother nods and then immediately follows my father, turning just as he reaches the door to hit me with a look I know all too well. Instantly my stomach goes sour.

"Good seeing you brother." He gives me a cocky smile and then glances to Allie. "I'll see you soon Miss Reynolds." He winks and then spins on his heel, walking out of the room without another glance in my direction.

Chapter Five

Samantha

"So whenever you receive new client information it is your responsibility to pull each document and file it accordingly. All fund transfers go here." Katherine moves the mouse and double clicks on yet another folder, further filling my already cluttered computer screen. "But always make sure that it's the original transaction. Any transactions past the initial buy out are to be sorted separately here." She clicks another file open, a spreadsheet taking the forefront among all the other applications and folders open.

"So how do I know the difference?" I ask, hoping my question doesn't strike her as odd. I am not sure if this is information I should know going in or if my question is perfectly justified.

"By the code." She points to a six digit number on the top left of the document lying in front of me on the desk. "They are all sorted by a sequence of numbers. I will draw you up a little cheat sheet to help you until you get a grasp on all of this. I know it can be a lot." She leans back in her chair next to me and gives me a cheeky smile.

"It is." I agree, pushing back slightly from my desk to swivel my chair towards her. "I was worried it was just me." I let out a sigh.

"Good heavens no." She shakes her head, the red bun on top not moving in the slightest as she does. "It took me ages to get all of this down. Of course, when I started here thirteen years ago things were a bit different."

"How long have you been working directly for Luke?" I ask, feeling comfortable enough to ask Katherine without fearing she will balk at my attempts to make small talk.

It may only be my first day but already I can tell that Katherine is a very mothering type of woman and from my experience in my few short hours with her, she has no problem slowing down for idle chit chat.

"Four years now." She smiles, the small wrinkles surrounding her blue eyes crinkling as she does. "He's a good boy." Her smile widens the more she speaks. "He's like one of my own. I love him like a son but respect him as a boss. I think you'll find he's fair and kind and he cares very much for the people working with him."

"He definitely seems nicer than I expected a Scott to be." I voice aloud, my heart immediately picking up speed as I realize what I have said.

"He's not like the other men in his family, that's for sure." She nods her head in agreement, clearly thinking nothing of my comment.

I immediately relax back into my chair, trying not to show the alarm that just rang through my body.

"What do you mean?" I ask curiously, crossing my arms in front of my chest.

"Let's just say that he's a bit of a black sheep. I don't want to be quoted speaking negatively of my new bosses." She gives a light chuckle, leaning forward to tap my knee with her small hand. "Just rest assured you are in good hands Miss Reynolds. Luke Scott is one of the good ones." She gives me a wink before pushing out of the chair next to me.

"Anyways, I think that just about does it for the day." She rolls the chair she was just occupying around the front of the desk to where it belongs. "I don't think Mr. Scott would think kindly to me keeping you here well past leaving time on your first day. He might accuse me of trying to scare you off." She laughs again, the genuine sound almost melodic.

"As if that would be possible." I laugh, returning her smile. "Thank you so much for all your help. Truly, I don't know how I would figure all this out without you."

"My pleasure dear. I will feel better leaving knowing that you are prepared and ready to do the job. It will make the transition much easier on all of us." She grabs the box full of her personal belongings that she packed up earlier today, resting it on her hip as she supports it with one arm.

"Can I help you with any of that?" I ask as she reaches for her purse.

"Oh no need." She shakes her head, draping the leather bag over her forearm. "I'm just going up a floor to drop these things off in my new office. I will see you tomorrow Allie." She nods and then spins on her heel, disappearing through the office door before I have a chance to speak again.

Looking to the empty doorway and then back down at my cluttered computer screen, I can't help but feel a bit overwhelmed by everything that has happened today, the amount of work I am expected to do just a small piece of that.

My mind immediately flashes back to earlier today; to the moment when Nicholas and Ryan were sitting within arm's length of me, so close I could have reached out and touched them. So long I have wondered what that would feel like and even now I am not sure I have fully processed the array of emotions that seem to be flooding through me.

Looking back to my computer, I rest my hand on top of the mouse and begin moving files into their appropriate folders. I know Katherine said I could go but honestly, going home when you have nothing to go home to is not really all that inviting. I have stared at the same four walls for weeks; I am in no rush to go back there right now.

Before long I am in lost to my work, organizing, and moving files into a system that better suits me. I know this job is a front, my means to get close to the Scott's, but that doesn't mean I don't have a façade to uphold. I need my work to at least be satisfactory enough that I can pretty well fly under the radar and draw as little attention to myself as possible.

The minutes slip by the further I delve into my work. I don't bother to look at the time; time really holds no value when all you have is time. When I finally do glance at the clock above my office door I jump slightly, not expecting to see Luke leaning in the doorway watching me.

"Sorry, I didn't mean to startle you." He gives me a smile, revealing a mouth full of perfectly straight white teeth.

It's the kind of smile that makes you melt a little. I find myself once again momentarily distracted by how incredibly attractive Luke is.

"I said your name but you didn't answer." He adds.
"Oh." I shake my head, not realizing how focused I must have been until just now. "Sorry about that." I laugh lightly at myself.

"What are you still doing here?" He asks, reminding me that I didn't actually check the time, distracted by his unexpected appearance.

Flicking my eyes to the clock above Luke, I see that it is already after eight in the evening.

"Sorry, I was trying to get some of these organized." I shake my head again, quickly trying to bring some sense to the files strewn out across my desk.

"You do realize that you have plenty of time to get settled? I don't expect you to work all day and night trying to play catch up." He lets out a light chuckle.

"Of course, I apologize. I just had a few things I wanted to finish up and I guess I lost track of time." I reach for my mouse, closing down the files I am done with before minimizing the others.

"No need to apologize." He makes no attempt to move from the doorway. "I just want to make sure you understand that it is not expected."

"I do, thank you." I push away from the desk, draping my purse over my shoulder. "I guess I should head out then." I finally look up, meeting his crystal gaze. The intensity behind his incredible eyes immediately makes me feel squeamish as I cross the office towards him.

"Do you have plans for dinner?" He asks, causing my movements to stall just feet from the door.

"Tonight?" The words come out riddled with surprise.

"Tonight." He confirms. "I mean, considering you worked such a long day the least I can do is feed you."

"Yeah, um, well I…" I have trouble finding a response which immediately frustrates me.

What is it about this man that throws me so far off my game? I have never met anyone that makes me as nervous as Luke Scott does.

"You're busy?" He phrases it like a question, rescuing me from my sudden inability to talk.

"Yeah. Busy." I confirm, not really sure what to think of his invitation.

"Maybe another time." He steps back from the doorway, allowing me to pass by him.

I try to ignore the way my breath catches as I squeeze past him into the hallway, or the way my heart accelerates as his incredible smell engulfs me. Everything about this man has me desperate to know more, see more, experience more.

Everything except for one crippling detail… He's a Scott.

"Goodnight Miss Reynolds." I can hear the smile in his voice as I pass by him without so much as a backwards glance.

"Goodnight Mr. Scott." I reply, quickly pushing my way out of the reception area and into the dimly lit hallway that leads to the elevators. I no more than reach the doors before his voice once again halts my movements.

"Miss Reynolds."

I slowly turn to find him walking towards me, yet another jaw dropping smile lighting up his handsome face. My mind is racing, using every ounce of its energy to determine what he is doing, how I should react, and most importantly, what the hell is wrong with me.

"You forgot your jacket." He gestures to the

material draped over his forearm before holding it out to me.

"Oh, right." I can't keep the heat from rushing to my cheeks as I take it from him, praying the entire time that he won't see the blush that I am sure is masking my entire face.

"Goodnight." He says again, lingering in front of me for what feels like an eternity before finally turning and walking away, leaving me standing in the hallway unable to comprehend why such an innocent encounter would have the ability to shake me to my very core.

Chapter Six

Samantha

"Don't tell me that brother of mine already has you working late on your second week?" I turn from my place in front of the copy machine to find Ryan standing just a couple of feet behind me, a stack of files in his arms.

"Not to worry, I actually think he has an adversity to how late I want to stay." I laugh lightly. "What do you have there?" I gesture to the files he's holding, just trying to make conversation.

While I was hoping to hear from Ryan much sooner than this, especially given how interested he seemed in me at lunch last week, I can't deny the thrill that runs through me that he's here now. I knew going in that worming my way into Ryan's world wouldn't be easy but I had hoped it would be a little faster moving then it has been thus far.

"New acquisitions." He shrugs. "Luke just finished these. Though I am starting to wonder if having an assistant that works all hours of the day and night didn't help him close these in record time." He gives me a cocky smile.

"I'm afraid that's all Luke." I return his smile, wishing he could feel the hatred flowing from every pore in my body.

Soon, I remind myself, widening my smile.
"I've been meaning to stop by and see you." He continues without acknowledging my words.
"You have?" I question, playing like I have no idea why.
"I believe you agreed to have dinner with me." He reminds me, not the least bit offended by my pretending that I forgot.
"I did do that didn't I?" I smile playfully.
"Well since we are both here, how about now?"
"Like right now?" I ask, confused and completely unprepared.
"Right now." He confirms with a smile. "I just need to drop these off at my father's office. What do you say; meet me in the lobby in about fifteen?" He asks.
"I'll do you one better. How about I walk up with you?" I say, having been dying for an excuse to go upstairs where Ryan and Nicholas's offices are since I started here.
"Works for me." His smile widens.
"Let me just put these on my desk." I pull the copies from the machine before turning back towards him.
"After you." He smiles, gesturing for me to go first.
Nodding, I slip past him, not sure if I am more excited or sick to my stomach at the thought of spending the evening in this man's company.

"So how long have you lived in Los Angeles?" Ryan asks, tilting his wine glass to his lips before taking a drink, his eyes not leaving my face as he does.

"Well I grew up in Bear River Wyoming." I lie, taking a drink of my own wine.

"Bear River?" He questions, clearly having never heard of such a place.

"Never heard of it?" I laugh, setting down my wine glass. "Don't worry, you aren't missing much. It's so small it's practically non-existent."

"So you didn't move to California until…"

"College." I finish his sentence. "Bit of a culture shock but I adapted." I laugh lightly, already feeling the heat from the wine flooding my face.

"Do your parents still live there, in Wyoming I mean?" He asks.

"Yes, I'm sure they will live there forever. You couldn't pay my dad to leave." I say, swallowing down the hard lump that forms in my throat at the lie.

"I can understand that. I doubt I could ever leave L.A.; at least not for any real amount of time." He immediately moves the conversation in another direction. "So what do you like to do for fun?"

His transition from one conversation to the next is a bit abrupt and sometimes makes little sense but I do my best to keep up without letting my annoyance show through. In just the short time we have been here it has become very clear to me that Ryan Scott is not a man to discuss matters of the heart, always changing the conversation before it can become to intimate.

"I don't have tons of hobbies." I finally answer his question after a long pause. "I love to read and paint. And the beach, I love the beach." I add.

"What's your favorite beach?" He leans back in his chair, his eyes still locked firmly on me.

"Well considering I have only been to Santa Monica, I guess that one."

"I'm sorry what?" He fakes like he's having trouble hearing me which I think is meant to come across as cute but really just sours the taste in my mouth further.

"Bear River, remember?" I laugh, gesturing to myself.

"Oh you haven't been to a beach until you've seen Palawan Beach in Singapore. It's set around these really dramatic limestone formations and has the whitest sand you'll probably ever see. The water is so blindingly blue it makes all other water look murky in comparison and has by far the best sunsets you will ever experience."

"Sounds like a beautiful place." I drain the remainder of my wine before placing the empty glass back down on the table.

"I must take you there." He says, his smile turning wildly wicked.

"Someday maybe." I'm not sure how else to respond so I casually blow off his statement.

"Why not today?" He cocks an eyebrow up at me.

"Um, because we can't." I say like it should be

pretty obvious.

"Why can't we?" He seems genuinely confused by my reluctance.

"Because a trip like that takes some planning I'm sure. Not to mention I have to work." I add on.

"One, you work for *my* company." He puts an emphasis on *my*. "And two, I can have the private jet fueled and ready to leave in an hour."

"You're crazy." I shake my head playfully at him, trying to play it off as he's joking when I know full well he is very serious.

It has never been more blindingly clear that Ryan Scott views nothing as out of the realm of possibility.

"I'm serious. Let's go." His cocky smile slides into place as our waitress reappears with the bottle of wine; topping off our glasses before silently excusing herself.

"I can't." I wait until she walks away before finally answering.

"You mean you won't. When you're with me Allie, can't isn't an option." He leans forward, his hand coming to a rest just above my knee underneath the flowing white linen that covers the table.

My heart immediately picks up speed as he squeezes firmly, the look in his eyes making my stomach twist. I have to play into this, I know I do. But it makes me ill to think about how far I may need to take this in order to gain access to Ryan's world.

"Fine, I won't. But not because I don't want too." I add on to lessen the blow. "I don't want to skip out on work before I have even completed two full weeks. Regardless of who owns the company, it's not the way I operate."

He leans back, the contact between us ceasing allowing me to relax slightly. Cocking his head to the side, he studies me for a long moment before a slow smile creeps across his handsome face.

"You're not like the typical women I take out." He finally speaks after several long moments of silence.

"Is that a bad thing?" I ask, not sure if it's a compliment or an insult.

"Quite the opposite actually." His brown eyes focus on my face as he takes in my reaction. "What do you say we get out of here?" He asks.

"Bored of me already Mr. Scott?" I joke, feeling a wave of panic ride through me.

"Oh no Miss Reynolds, with you I'm just getting started." His words don't just hold a promise, they also hold a command.

As he stares back at me, waiting for my reply, I realize that if I let him in that easily, he will discard me as quickly as yesterday's trash. While I am fully aware that there will come a point where he will expect more, I also know that making him work for it will keep him interested longer and hopefully buy me a pass behind the scenes for more than just one night.

"I suppose I should be heading home. I have to be back at the office in just a few short hours." I retrieve my purse from the back of my chair without so much as an acknowledgement of the statement he just made.

"Oh, come on. The night is still young." He insists; clearly not ready to let me go that easily.

"To you maybe." I give him a shy smile.

"Well at least let me drive you home." He scrambles to his feet just as I stand, clearly thrown off by how quickly the night is ending.

"Please." I place my hand on his chest as he steps

directly in front of me. "Stay, finish your wine." I look up into his dark eyes. "Thank you for the lovely dinner." I push up on my tip toes and place a feather light kiss to his cheek.

"Goodnight Ryan." I say, pulling back and giving him a slight nod.

"Allie." He steps back, allowing me to pass.

Despite my elation over how disappointed he seems, I manage to hold myself together until I exit the restaurant a few short moments later. The laughter building inside of me spills out the second the cool night air surrounds me.

The look on his face when I stood from that table was priceless. Hell, I would bet money this is the first time he has ever taken a girl to dinner and not taken her home to his bed afterward. And to think, he thought he could win me over by what, skirting me off to some foreign country and showing me what his millions can buy?

A weird sense of satisfaction settles over me on the cool walk home. I know it's a small win but it's the first win I have gotten since setting this plan into motion. It's something. I don't know why but I just expected that the moment I started working for Sco-Tech my plan would just sort of magically work itself out. I didn't realize just how difficult it would actually be to infiltrate the illusive world of Ryan Scott.

Getting just one step closer, no matter how small the step, feels like an amazing victory. I still may have no idea what I am looking for or what to do if I find anything on Ryan or Nicholas but knowing that I might just get the opportunity to find out, makes everything I have sacrificed these last two years to get here worth it.

Nothing will bring my family back, I know that. Nothing will right the wrongs done to them, I also know that. But I still believe that I can find peace in the eye of the storm. I believe that I can bring at least some sense of justice to what happened to my brother, and my parents. At the very least, I will find a way to bring Ryan Scott to his knees.

He may view me as just another quest, another woman to conquer, but he couldn't be more wrong. I am going to make Ryan Scott mine and then, I'm going to destroy him.

Chapter Seven

Luke

"Boy that assistant of yours sure knows how to make a man work for it." My brother's voice startles me from behind and I turn my head to see him waltzing out onto the patio where I am sitting; watching the storm roll in over the ocean.

I want to comment on the fact that he just comes right in like he owns the place but I am too distracted by his comment to get past anything but that.

"I'm sorry?" I question, taking a long drag of my beer, not attempting to move from my lounging position.

"Allie." He smiles, flopping down in the chair next to me, propping his feet up onto the unlit stone fire pit in front of us. "That girl is something." He licks his lips and makes a pleased sound.

"Ryan." I warn, knowing he already knows how I feel about these types of situations, especially where my new assistant is concerned.

I wish I could say her being my assistant is all that bothers me about this, unfortunately that would be a lie. I can't deny the pull I feel towards the young Miss Reynolds. There's just something about her.

"Relax. She's playing right now, but rest assured I will get her there." He says, his confidence unwavering.

A wave of relief washes over me when I realize what he's saying.

"Shot you down did she?" I take another long gulp of beer, not able to contain my pleased smile.

"Shit. No one shoots me down. She just needs a slower approach. Though I must say, I've never had a girl refuse a trip to an exotic beach before. Hell, usually all I have to do is mention the private jet and they are tripping over themselves to get on board. But this one, she barely batted an eye." He rubs his forehead.

"A woman that you can't buy? What is this world coming to?" I say sarcastically, rolling my eyes as I turn back towards the water.

"Fuck you Luke." He pulls my attention back to him. "Why do you always have to be such a dick?"

"Not indulging in your childish bullshit is not being a dick. I have no choice but to tolerate you because you're my brother, that doesn't mean I have to play sunshine and rainbows." I meet his narrowed stare.

I can see the surprise on his face, though he does relatively well masking it. It's not like I haven't said the same thing to him on countless other occasions over the past ten years and yet he still seems shocked when I more or less tell him to fuck off.

"See, this is what I get for trying to bond with my brother. What the fuck man?" He pushes into a stand.

"No this is what you get for barging into my home unannounced for the sole purpose of rubbing it in my face that you were out with Miss Reynolds tonight." I reply dryly, not attempting to move.

"Last time I checked, Dad owns this house." He points out like so many times before.

"Last time I checked, he also owns the apartment in the city that you call home. You don't see me just barging in on you do you?" I lash, sick of his bullshit.

This whole thing with Allie has taken my ability to somewhat tolerate my brother and completely obliterated it.

"Yeah well it will *all* be mine soon enough." There is a threat behind his words, as if his threats scare me at all.

"And I am sure you'll destroy it all, just like you do everything you touch." I holler after him as he crosses the patio towards the back door that leads inside.

"Don't worry, I'll start by destroying that sweet little ass assistant of yours. Have a fucking awesome night brother." He spits, disappearing inside before I can respond.

I tip my beer up and drain the bottle empty before tossing it at the four foot stone wall that surrounds the outdoor living space. The bottle shatters, causing tiny shards of dark stained glass to spray just feet from where I am sitting.

Leave it to Ryan to disrupt what little time I have to myself. The vision of him and Allie together flashes in my mind and an instant chill runs through me. As much as I don't want to, I know I am going to have to talk to Allie about Ryan. I hate to think it's come to this but he has left me no other choice.

"You got a minute?" I knock lightly on the door frame of Allie's office, causing her to look up from her computer screen and hit me with a sweet smile.

"Sure." She replies, gesturing for me to come in. "Is everything okay?" She asks, causing me to realize I must be wearing my dread for this conversation on my face.

Closing the office door, I quickly cross the space and take a seat across from her before answering. "I actually wanted to talk to you about Ryan." I say, watching the color fall from her face slightly.

"Okay." She immediately seems nervous which oddly enough makes my attraction to her even greater.

There is something so incredibly fucking sweet about this girl, especially when her pale cheeks flood with pink and she can't seem to hold my gaze. It drives me fucking crazy, in a good way of course.

"I know you went out with him last night." I start, not sure exactly how to word this. "And there is no policy saying that you can't." I reassure her when I see the panic flash across her features. "But as your boss, I wanted to at least express to you my concern."

"Okay." She replies weakly, waiting for me to continue.

"You have expressed interest in moving up within this company and honestly, based on what I have seen, you definitely possess the skills to do so. I would hate to see your career goals derailed over someone like Ryan. Please forgive me for being so blunt but my brother is not someone you want to get tied up with. If you are getting involved with him thinking it will be anything beyond a hookup, I'm afraid you're mistaken. I realize this is completely unprofessional of me but I like you Miss Reynolds, you seem like a really bright girl, and I really don't want to see you fall victim to Ryan like so many other past employees have." I say, stopping to gauge her reaction.

When she doesn't respond immediately, I continue.

"I won't tell you that you can't see him and there will be no repercussions on my end as long as it does not affect your work. I just felt like I needed to at least let you know what you're getting yourself into." I finish, meeting her gaze as she nervously twirls her hair around her finger.

"I... I appreciate that." She finally manages to stutter out.

"Well, I will let you get back to work." I finally say after a few moments of heavy silence. "I hope you will really think about what I've said." I add, standing from the chair, not wanting to drag out the awkwardness that seems to have settled into the space around us.

"I will. Thank you." She gives me a weak smile just moments before I exit her office.

Pushing my way inside my own office, I shut the door and immediately cross the space, collapsing into the chair behind my desk. What the fuck is wrong with me? This girl takes me from a strong confident business man to feeling like a scared little teenage boy in one fucking look.

"Fuck." I lean forward, my elbows coming to a rest on top of the desk as I drop my head into my hands.

This girl has me so all over the place and I have barely even spoken to her outside of spreadsheets, account verifications, and scheduling. There's just something there. Something I can't explain and yet am dying to explore.

I am not Ryan. I remind myself. I do not hook up with co-workers; especially not someone I work so closely with. It's just not my style. And yet, this girl has me willing to throw every rule I have out of the window just for the

chance to get to know her on a real level.
I am so fucked…

Chapter Eight

Samantha

"Can I call you a car Miss?" I jump slightly from where I am standing inside the lobby of The Regency, an upscale apartment complex where I told Ryan to pick me up for our date tonight.

I turn towards the man from my place next to the window, trying my best not to seem too suspicious.

"I'm just waiting on a friend of mine." I smile politely.

"Didn't want this friend of yours to know where you really live?" The gray haired man gives me an understanding smile. "Don't worry; you'd be surprised how many people claim to live here. Los Angeles is a fickle place. You aren't anybody unless you pretend to be somebody." He reaches out, placing a wrinkled hand on my shoulder.

"Am I that obvious?" I let out a nervous laugh before finally meeting the older man's eyes. They are a crisp blue, almost the same color as Luke's, though they lack the intensity that his seem to carry.

"No actually." He drops his hand, shaking his head as he turns to stand next to me, looking out of the front window of the hotel style lobby. "I just know every tenant and most of their guests and I don't recall ever seeing you here before. I took a guess."

"Good guess." I glance at the side of his face before also turning my attention to the outside world.

"Well whoever this friend is, he's one lucky man." I can hear the genuine kindness in his voice which immediately soothes some of the nerves raging through me at the current moment.

"You don't think it's too much?" I ask, glancing down at my fitted black cocktail dress and four inch matching heels. I have no idea where Ryan is taking me and therefore had no idea what to wear.

"I think you look lovely dear." He glances at me out of the corner of his eye.

"Thank you." I answer immediately, for whatever reason just needing a little reassurance.

This has to be one of the strangest conversations I have had and yet it feels completely natural, like I have known this man for years.

"I think your friend has arrived." He pulls my attention back outside and I immediately spot the expensive red sports car that pulls up and parks directly in front of the building.

"How did you…" I trail off when he turns towards me and gives me a wide tooth smile.

"I told you, I know everyone that lives in this building and most of their guests and I can tell you with complete certainty that I have never seen a car like that here before."

"You're good…" I pause, glancing to his name tag.

"Charles." I tack on. "Thank you." I give him a sweet smile. "For not ratting me out and for being so nice."

"It was my pleasure dear." He nods, leading me to the front door.

Without another word he pushes it open and steps out onto the sidewalk, waiting for me to step through before giving me one last smile and disappearing back inside.

By the time I turn back around, Ryan is out of the car and crossing the sidewalk towards me, his eyes trailing down my body before finally meeting my face, a satisfied grin turning up the corners of his mouth.

"You look gorgeous." He smiles, leaning in to place a brief kiss to my cheek. I smile, trying my best not to seem too repulsed by his touch.

"Thank you." I get out weakly before following him to the passenger side of the sports car.

I try once again not to cringe when his hand falls to the small of my back as he guides me into the car.

It's strange really, having someone as rich and attractive as Ryan have the exact opposite effect on me that I am sure he has on every other woman he comes in contact with. I guess the difference between them and me is that I know behind his smooth seductive smile and deep brown eyes lurks his true self.

Climbing into the driver's side, he fires the car to life, revving the engine slightly in a poor attempt to impress me with a car that probably costs more money than my childhood home did. Trying to push away my annoyance, I turn towards him just as he pulls the car out onto the busy street and hits the gas hard.

"So can I ask where we are going?" I take a moment to actually look at his attire which immediately confirms that I made the right choice with the dress.

He's wearing black suit pants with a gray button down shirt, the top two buttons open revealing a white shirt underneath. He seems casual enough but still screams wealth. It's almost like it seeps from his every pore, announcing to the world that he is someone of importance. I guess that depends on what you define as important. I see it as nothing more than another reason to despise him.

"You'll see." He raises his eyebrows up and down as he throws me a quick side glance before turning his attention back out the windshield.

He whips and speeds through traffic like he owns the road, tapping on the steering wheel in impatience and making a few noises of displeasure when someone gets in front of him that doesn't drive fast enough. By the time we reach the water line nearly an hour later, I am so on edge my stomach muscles feel sore from clenching the entire drive over.

When Ryan pulls the car off just to the left of a private dock entrance, I don't hesitate pushing the door open and immediately climbing out, eager to escape the confines of the vehicle. Shutting the door, I look around at our surroundings, noticing immediately a huge difference between the boats that were docked at the front of the marina versus the ones now stretched before me.

These aren't just boats, at least not the kind of boat that someone like me encounters in their lifetime. Stretched out in front of me are some of the largest and fanciest water vessels I have ever seen. Ryan slips his arm over my shoulder, a pleased smile pulling up the corners of his mouth. He's clearly pleased with my reaction, though he has no idea that what he views as me being impressed is really just me being in very unfamiliar territory and not really sure how to react.

"They're amazing right?" He leads me down a small path before stopping in front of the massive gate that blocks the private dock from all the others, thankfully dropping his arm from my shoulder to slide it open.

"I've never seen anything like it." I admit, stepping through the gate after he gestures for me to go first.

"This is probably my favorite place in the world." He admits, stepping past me to lead me down a long trail of massive yachts and luxurious houseboats.

I find myself looking down at my feet for most of the walk, trying to make sure my thin heels do not catch in the small gaps between the boards that make up the dock. If it wasn't obvious before that walking in shoes like this is completely unnatural to me, it sure as hell is now. When I do finally glance back up after several moments of looking down, I see Ryan watching me from the end of the dock, an amused smile lighting up his face.

It's weird, in the pale light of the setting sun he almost seems like a normal guy. Shrouded by orange and yellow and backed by the reflection of the water, for a brief moment I can see why so many girls fall at his feet. With a large smile, he extends his hand to me the moment I reach him.

"Welcome to *Scott's Paradise*." He says, referring to the name etched along the back of the massive yacht docked at the very end of the strip directly in front of us.

"This is yours?" I ask the obvious question simply trying to play into his clear excitement.

"It is." He confirms, helping me on board before climbing on behind me.

The yacht is massive in size, stretching out for several yards in front of me, the entire floor resembling a hard wood that someone might use in a house. There is a curved couch that extends several feet along the railing to my right and six lounge chairs to my left, a small bar directly next to them. In the center is a large awning, a four person dining table and chairs located below it which I immediately realize is already set with two place settings, a bottle of wine chilling in the center of the table. Glancing back at Ryan, he is watching me intensely, taking in my reaction.

"Do you like it?" He asks, stepping up next to me.

"It's beautiful." I answer truthfully.

I immediately envision what this would feel like if the man doing it for me was not Ryan Scott. If I were here in another life and time, and this moment was actually as magical as I imagine it could be. My mind briefly flips to Luke and I can't help the heat the floods through me at the thought.

"Come." Ryan pulls me from my daydream and I glance up to find him gesturing towards the set table.

Smiling, I immediately follow him to the center of the deck, sliding into the chair that he pulls out for me. I open my mouth to ask a question but then immediately close it when two young waiters suddenly appear from below deck, each one carrying a silver platter.

One sets his platter in front of Ryan, the other in front of me, both pulling the lids off simultaneously revealing a beautiful arrangement of fish and vegetables drizzled in what looks like some sort of glaze.

"Thank you." I look up at the freckled face server who can't be any older than I am, and I'm not referring to how old I claim to be.

If I had to guess I would say he's just recently graduated high school. I can't help but wonder how one becomes a cook or server, whichever he actually is, on a private yacht for a very wealthy family but before I can think too much of it Ryan clears his throat, pulling my attention back to him as the two young men disappear as quickly as they appeared.

"I know you're not a fan of raw fish." He jokes, referring to our conversation about sushi the first day we met. "I hope you don't have the same adversity to cooked fish."

"Not at all." I shake my head, plastering on the fakest smile I can muster. "It looks amazing. You really didn't need to go through all the trouble though." I gesture around the boat, for the first time realizing that there are soft white lights draped from the canopy above us, providing a soft intimate lighting.

"No trouble at all." He smiles, pouring us each a glass of wine before lifting his glass.

"What are we drinking to?" I ask, retrieving my wine glass as well.

"You." He gives me a wide smile. "Thank you for agreeing to join me tonight."

"Thank you for inviting me." I smile, finding some type of sick satisfaction knowing that he has no idea what my true intentions are.

To him I am just another quest; another woman to mark down on what I am sure is a very extensive list. Knowing my real motives, gives me this weird pleasure. Like knowing a secret that no one else knows, I revel in the power that gives me over him.

Most of the meal is eaten in silence and while the company leaves a bit to be desired, the food is exquisite. Ryan stops every few minutes to make a comment about the meal and how beautiful the night is, keeping the conversation light throughout the course of our meal. Before long, the waiters reappear and clear away our empty plates, replacing our empty bottle of wine with a new one.

Ryan refills his glass and then mine before settling back in his seat and taking a long drink. Not sure what else to do, I mirror his actions and take another drink myself, though I know I should stop soon considering I can already feel the effects of the wine working my purpose for being here out of the forefront of my mind.

When someone says I am only human, there couldn't be a truer statement. I find that to be exactly the case here. Sure, it's easy to hate Ryan after everything he's done but even I would be naïve to say that I am completely immune to his obvious charm. Add on four glasses of wine and he becomes more endearing by the moment. Even still, my resolve holds true.

"So, tell me a little more about yourself." I finally speak after a few long moments of silence.

"What do you want to know?" He asks, taking another drink of wine.

"I don't know. Tell me your deepest secret." I give him a challenging look, my smile playful.

"I would but then I'd have to kill you." He hits me with intense eyes and for a moment I believe his words.

Something about the heat behind his gaze, even if he is smiling, tells me not to underestimate what this man is capable of.

"Fine." I playfully pout. "Then tell me your biggest regret."

"Not meeting you sooner." He immediately

answers, a sly smile stretching across his face.

"Ha. Ha." I sigh sarcastically. "Seriously. Tell me your biggest regret."

"A man like me does not go through life without accumulating a rather large list of regrets." He sets down his wine glass on the table and crosses his arms in front of his chest.

"Well then pick one." I push.

"Why do you want to know so badly?" He raises an eyebrow at me.

"Because I want to get to know you. I find that a person's mistakes and regrets will tell you a lot more about who they are then anything else."

"Fair enough." He picks up his wine glass and drains the contents, clearly thinking over my statement. "If I had to pick my biggest regret, it would be getting into the car with one of my fraternity brothers my freshman year of college. We had been drinking and we ended up in a pretty severe accident."

"Really?" My intrigue is not fake; I truly want to know how he tells this story, knowing immediately that he's talking about Sean. "What happened?"

"Most of the night is pretty foggy. We had been bar hopping, you know, the normal college crap. Sean, which was his name." He adds, causing my heart to hammer wildly against my ribcage. "He wanted to take my dad's Ferrari out for a spin. I knew it was a bad idea considering how much he had been drinking but I agreed anyways."

"So he was driving?" I ask, immediately correcting the statement as to not draw suspicion to my comment. "I mean, after he had been drinking all night?" I tack on.

"Yeah, I know it was stupid. Anyways, we got a ways out of the city and Sean really wanted to see what the car could do so he gunned it. We had to have been going well over a hundred miles an hour when he hit a curve in the road too fast and lost control." He pauses, not realizing that just feet from him I am trying to stop myself from lunging over the table at him.

How dare he...

How dare he turn the accident on Sean and use it to play the victim. I can feel my restraint wavering and I do my best to hold it together as I push him to continue.

"That's horrible. Were you badly hurt?" I ask, like I have no idea of the outcome of the crash.

"I got knocked around pretty bad. Luckily, it wasn't anything too serious. Unfortunately, Sean was killed instantly." He acts like this is such a painful thing for him to talk about but I can quickly see through it. I know better.

"I'm so sorry Ryan." It takes everything I have to say those words and even though I know it's necessary, I can't control the sick feeling that forms in my stomach as they leave my mouth.

"It was a long time ago." He shrugs. "Worst part of it all was that the cops tried to pin the accident on me. Not only had I lost one of my best friends but then I had to answer for his actions." He shakes his head, not realizing that he just verbalized the fact that he viewed this being worse than his friend dying.

"Well clearly you weren't though. Surely they were able to prove that." I say, refilling my wine glass and taking another long gulp.

Lord knows I need it right now. Every part of my body is fighting against my natural instinct to defend my brother and what the man sitting in front of me did to him.

"It all worked out in the end." He gives me a

lopsided grin and shakes his head. "Okay enough of that." He sets his wine glass back down and quickly stands, his actions so abrupt they catch me off guard.

"Would you like to dance?" He smiles down at me, holding his hand out to me.

"Now?" I question, looking around, wishing there were a way to decline.

The last thing I want right now is to be forced into the arms of this man, especially after the ridiculous tale he just told.

"Why not?" He questions, his smile widening.

Despite the fact that it goes against everything inside of me, I take his hand and allow him to pull me to my feet. He leads me to an open portion of the deck just a few feet from the table and pulls me into his arms, my shoulders stiffening slightly at the close proximity of our bodies.

"Do you make a habit out of dancing with no music?" I try to keep up the charade, knowing the only way to get vengeance for Sean is to do exactly that.

The thought strengthens my resolve and I look up to meet his gaze, letting the effects of the wine flood through me and ease what I am about to do.

"Who needs music? I just wanted to hold you in my arms." He lays on a line I'm sure he's used countless times before.

I let him believe I bought it, hook line and sinker. I smile up at him, wrapping my hand around the back of his head. With the height of my heels, I only stand about four inches below him. Using this to my advantage, I guide his face downwards with my fingers threaded through the back of his hair until just a couple of inches separate our lips.

Closing my eyes, I lean forward, closing the gap between us. The moment his lips meet mine, I can feel the bile rising in my throat. I try to shift my focus, imagine that he's someone else, but as his tongue skirts along my bottom lip requesting access to my mouth, I'm not sure how much more I can take.

But then it happens… Luke's face flashes through my mind and I find the focal point I need. I deepen the kiss without another thought, my hand tightening in the back of Ryan's hair as his needy hands roam my back, pulling me tightly into him as his lips work against mine.

Chapter Nine

Luke

The moment the two people on the deck of my father's yacht come into view, I freeze, unable to look away from the scene unfolding in front of my very eyes. When I came here looking for my father, the last thing I expected to find was my brother locked in a passionate embrace with Allie.

I thought for sure my warning would have worked. She seems so uninterested in him and yet, here she is, kissing him like her life somehow depends on it. I just can't seem to understand why.

Ryan pulls her closer, his hands skirting down her back before clamping down on her hips. The sight is enough to make my stomach twist viciously. I know I should walk away. I should walk away and pretend like I didn't see a thing. Allie is a big girl; she can make her own decisions. But knowing what I should do and what I am capable of doing are two very different things.

Before I even realize my own actions, I step up onto the deck of the yacht and loudly clear my throat, the two people in front of me immediately breaking apart to look in my direction.

"Luke." Ryan immediately speaks. "What are you doing here?" He keeps his voice casual for Allie but deep down I know he is pissed that I interrupted.

Smiling, I nod, knowing it will only further fuel his anger which is exactly what I want to do at this moment.

"Sorry to interrupt." I flick my eyes to Allie whose cheeks are a deep crimson, her eyes focused downward as if she's afraid to meet my gaze. "I was looking for Dad. I thought he would be here tonight." I continue, turning my attention back to Ryan.

"Well as you can see, he's not." Ryan gestures around.

"No matter, you can help me." I smile, seeing the fury that continues to grow behind Ryan's eyes.

He thinks that I am doing this purposely and while that's not entirely true, a small part of me is greatly enjoying taking a jab at him. It's not like he's not doing the exact same thing to me by being here with Allie.

"I'm kind of in the middle of something here brother. Can't it wait?" He asks, darting his eyes to Allie who is looking anywhere but at me or Ryan.

"Actually, I should probably go." Her soft words pull both of our attention to her as she turns towards Ryan.

"You don't have to do that." He insists, clearly not ready for her to leave.

"I know, but I really should be heading back." She insists, stepping past him to grab her small wristlet purse from the table before crossing the space back towards us.

"Well at least let me call you a car." He reaches out and tucks a stray strand of her hair away from her face, the action winding me, like a punch to my gut.

What the hell is wrong with me?

"No need. I can call a cab." She says, leaning forward to lay a brief kiss to his cheek. "We will talk later." She pats her palm lightly against his chest before turning towards me. "Luke." She nods, blushing again the moment her eyes meet mine.

"Miss Reynolds." I nod in return, addressing her professionally.

She quickly passes me, her eyes once again meeting mine for just a fraction of a second as she does, and then she's gone, disappearing into the darkness.

"What the fuck Luke?" Ryan's voice completely changes the moment he's sure Allie is out of earshot.

"What?" I play innocent, crossing the deck to where the two clearly had dinner.

Picking up the half empty wine bottle, I put it to my mouth and take a large drink before turning back towards Ryan.

"Pulled out the big guns did you?" I ask, looking at the wine label. "How does Dad feel about you drinking his private stock?" I ask, setting the bottle back onto the table.

"Are you fucking kidding me right now?" His eyes are wide like he can't believe my nerve. "What the fuck was that Luke?" He gestures to where Allie just exited a few moments ago.

"Well since both you and our father refuse to answer your phones, you really left me no other choice." I finally answer him.

"This has nothing to do with anything other than Allie. You're pissed that she was here." He accuses.

"I actually had no idea that you were out with Miss Reynolds tonight." I answer truthfully. "I told you, I came here looking for Dad. I have a few important details I need to discuss with him about the Cyntech buy out."

"Dad never comes here and you know it." He bites.

"Well considering I had already checked his house and the office, I thought it was worth a shot. As I said, I have some very important information on Cyntech."

"And it couldn't wait until morning?" He spits, clearly finding my timing suspect.

"Actually, no. I mean, unless he's okay with us being cut out by Thomas Harding." I answer casually with a shrug.

"What the fuck does Harding have to do with anything?" He bites.

"Only that his company made a play to outbid us under the table. I have a contact at Cyntech that strongly advised we close in and make a better offer before they sign tomorrow morning. I need to draw up the contracts and have Dad get in touch with them to close this deal before Harding pulls the rug right out from underneath us." I explain.

"Who knew Harding had such a backbone? I'm actually kind of impressed." Ryan nods in appreciation, my news somewhat distracting him from his anger at me for interrupting his date. "I'll get in touch with Dad." He nods, crossing the deck to retrieve his phone from the table.

"I will draft another contract and leave the numbers blank until I hear from one of you. And Ryan." I turn, pinning my eyes directly on his. "Don't fuck this up. I need a phone call in the next hour if you expect me to have time to cover all the bases before you make the proposal to Cyntech."

"I'm not stupid Luke." He doesn't try to hide his displeasure over my comment. "Dad is working me into the

CEO position for a reason."

"Then maybe you should start showing me what those reasons are because for the life of me, all I see is an immature spoiled brat who can't prioritize business over getting some." I spit, quickly exiting the yacht before he can reply.

I try to shake off the image that seems embedded in my brain; the sight of Allie and Ryan locked together still so fresh in my mind. While I disapprove of my brother's antics with women employed by ScoTech, I have never really cared before now. There's something about *this* woman. Something that makes me want to spare her the wrath that follows a relationship with my brother. But even I know that's not all there is too it.

My stomach tightens at the thought of what might have happened here tonight had I not shown up looking for my father. Would she have slept with him? Would she have willing entered into his bed after everything I told her yesterday?

It just doesn't make any sense. She seems completely uninterested in Ryan and yet, she continues to go out with him. I can tell by the way she looks at him that her hearts not in it. She doesn't look at him with the same intensity that I see in her eyes when she looks at me. He doesn't evoke the rush of blood to her cheeks the way I do or cause the nervous ticks that in just two short weeks have proven capable of bringing me to my fucking knees.

I know there's more to this, though I am fearful that a part of me is just looking for a way to justify her actions. Maybe Ryan is truly who she wants and I am so blinded by my own lust for her that I am just seeing what I want to see.

Either way, one thing couldn't be clearer; I have got to get Allie Reynolds out from under my skin.

Chapter Ten

Samantha

"Miss Reynolds." I hear Luke's voice behind me and turn just in time to see him step inside the small employee break room that sits at the end of the hall.

"Mr. Scott." I nod, turning back around to finish making my cup of hot tea.

Dropping a teaspoon of sweetener into the small white cup, I try to seem completely unaffected by his presence. It's only awkward if I make it so, right?

"I didn't know you were a tea drinker." He steps up next to me, giving me no choice but to look in his direction.

Like so many times before, the moment those crystal blues hit me a jolt of electricity shoots down my spine, causing me to shiver slightly.

"I find it soothing." I answer weakly, looking back down to my cup of tea as I stir it.

"Is there something you need soothing from?" He asks his question laced with an underlying statement.

I know without a doubt he's referring to Ryan even

though his tone remains smooth and unaffected by emotion.

While neither of us has spoken about what he witnessed Saturday night, I can tell that it is very much at the forefront of his mind, even if he doesn't say so. I can feel the tension between us, a heaviness that has always been there but has grown steadily more apparent throughout the course of the day.

"Just a long day." I sigh, not sure how else to respond.

"Monday tends to be that way around here." He agrees, waiting until I turn towards him, cup in hand, before continuing. "I wanted to let you know that I will be going out of town for the next couple of days." He starts.

"Oh." The word falls from my lips unintentionally and I can't help the disappointment that seems to settle over me at the thought of being here without him.

I know it sounds weird that I would feel this way after such a short period of time but Luke is somewhat of a safety blanket for me. He has this way of grounding me and keeping me calm, even when everything else seems to be spinning out of control. And he does it without doing anything. Just being near him seems to give me peace. It's the oddest feeling for someone like me who has found very little peace over the past eight years.

"I was hoping that you would be able to accompany me." He adds on, pulling my gaze back to his face.

"What?" I blurt, not sure how to react.

"We are trying to close a deal with a small tech business on the East Coast. The CEO and primary stock holder is proving rather difficult to sway due to other competitors advances. I could use someone with your talents to help me make sure when it's all said and done, he ends up on our side of the playing field."

"Talents?" I question, not sure what to make of the

comment.

"Sometimes it takes a woman's touch." He gives me a sweet smile which immediately brings one to my own face as well.

"Is that so?" I laugh lightly.

"It is. Grumpy old men tend to have a hell of a lot harder time saying no to a pretty woman then to someone like me." He shakes his head on a light laugh. "Do you think you could make it work?"

"You're the boss, Mr. Scott. I will do whatever you need me to." I respond. "When would we be leaving?"

"The private jet will fly us out tonight." He says, laughing when my eyes go wide.

"Tonight?"

"In three hours to be exact." He laughs again. "You're welcome to go ahead and wrap up whatever you are working on and head home to pack. I will have a car pick you up at seven sharp."

"Actually, can I just meet you there?" I ask, knowing that if he shows up where I claim to live, he will find that I don't actually live there.

While I succeeded in fooling Ryan on my place of residence, I doubt I could manage to get to my real home, pack, and then be able to make it to the Regency by seven considering it's nearly five now. Not to mention there is something so different about deceiving Ryan than there is Luke. Luke is different and while I know lying to him is inevitable, I don't want to do it when it's avoidable.

When this all blows up, because it eventually will, I would like to contain the blast radius as much as possible. People are going to get hurt, one way or another, but if I can keep Luke from being one of those people, then that's exactly what I am going to do.

"It's actually a private air strip and gaining access is not as easy as you might think. However, if it's easier, you can just meet me back here once you've had a chance to pack and we can head over together."

"Okay, that should work." I agree, knowing that my actual apartment is much closer than the Regency and I should have no trouble getting there and then back here in time.

"How should I pack?" I ask, having no idea what type of attire is going to be required for this trip.

"We're meeting with the board of Cyntech first thing tomorrow morning; your normal work attire should suffice. I would suggest bringing at least two professional outfits as we may be there for a couple of days. Tomorrow night we have reservations at Sachkets for drinks. I would suggest a nice cocktail dress or something similar. Our time there will hinge on how everything goes."

"Got it." I nod, my stomach already swirling at the thought of spending two days alone with Luke on the complete opposite side of the country.

"Meet me in the lobby at seven." He instructs, pushing away from the counter and crossing the small space towards the door. Turning just inside the doorframe, my stomach twists tighter when his eyes once again meet mine. "And thank you." He adds, a half smile pulling up one side of his mouth.

"For what?" I ask, confused by his comment.

"For agreeing to accompany me. Typically I would do this alone but something tells me I am going to need you." His smile widens causing a fluttering sensation to swarm my chest.

"Of course." I force a smile, despite the weakness

that seems to have formed in my knees at his words.

It might just be my imagination but I swear he put an emphasis on the word *need* and as he throws me another nod and quickly disappears down the hall. It takes everything I have to reel in my nerves and shake off the feeling that thought leaves me with.

I know better than to get involved with Luke. Even if he wanted it to, I could never deceive him that way. I could never let myself be with him knowing every single thing he knows about me is actually a lie. Hell, he doesn't even know my real name.

And while it's easy to get lost in the fantasy of what this situation could be like, I know that at the end of the day it's just that; a fantasy. Luke Scott could never want a woman like me. And since when have I cared if someone wanted me?

Therein lies my real problem. Luke stirs something in me, something that makes me feel almost normal. When he looks into my eyes, I am no longer *this* person. I am no longer part of this reality. I am simply a woman; a woman who longs for the man staring back at her, a woman who dreams of experiencing the ultimate fairytale; the handsome man swooping in and rescuing her from her damned fate to ride her off into the sunset where they will live happily ever after.

Closing my eyes, I take a deep breath and push the thought away. For the first time in a very long time I find myself wanting something beyond my revenge. I think that's the most unsettling part for me; knowing that the person capable of making me feel this way is tied directly to my road to vengeance.

There's no way I walk away from this situation a winner. No matter the outcome, I've already lost too much to ever consider myself victorious. But the thought that at the end of this I might have a chance at a normal life is something I have never considered before.

At least not until Luke.

He makes me long for a life I thought was out of my reach. He makes me want so much more for myself and yet, I hardly know him. It's not about what he has done but rather, how he makes me feel. It's in the simple everyday actions that I find this to be the truest.

Just being in the same room as him, feeling his eyes on my face, is enough to show me that beyond all the hatred and anger, the lies and deceit, there is a woman that still longs for the one thing everyone wishes to find; love.

Chapter Eleven

Samantha

I can't believe I'm actually here; New York. I knew coming here would be emotional, considering this is where Sean died, but I was absolutely not prepared for how good it feels being so far away from the West Coast, almost like existing in a completely different world.

I cross the space of my large hotel bedroom, which is included in the penthouse suite, to the massive set of double windows that sit along the back wall. I can't imagine what a room like this cost but considering its location in the heart of the city, I would say staying here one night is more than I make in a month. The thought is a bit nauseating really.

What is it with rich people throwing their money away on unnecessary things? Would it be so bad to just stay in a normal hotel room like a regular person? Even still, I can't deny the beauty of my lush surroundings or the amazing view of the city that stretches out before me. The view is breathtaking and completely intimidating at the same time.

When Luke first mentioned the trip, I just assumed I would be staying in my own room. I never imagined we would be staying in a hotel room that looks more like an apartment or that I would be sleeping in a room just feet from where Luke will be staying. The thought makes my stomach twist tightly; mainly because it excites me but more because that excitement terrifies me.

I hear a light knock on my door, jumping slightly as the noise startles me.

"Yes." I manage to croak out, my voice breaking at the end.

"Hey." Luke gives me a sweet smile the moment he steps into the half open doorway.

"Hey." I smile, turning inward to face him.

"I have a few things I need to work on before our meeting tomorrow. I'm going to head down to the lounge. I just wanted to make sure you have everything you need." He glances at the view behind me before meeting my gaze again. "It's incredible isn't it?" He gestures to the window, not allowing me to answer his first question before asking another.

"It really is." I agree, turning slightly to look back out over the city.

"I remember when I used to come here with my mom as a kid." He says, pausing.

I tense when I realize that he has not only entered the room completely but is now standing just two feet from me, sharing in my view of New York.

"She would always make sure whenever we came here with my father on business that we got the highest room she could find in the city." He continues. "After the sun would set, we would sit next to the windows and look out over the city. Each time she would pick a building and then she would tell me a story of how it came to be. She loved history." He gives me a side glance, answering my question before I can ask.

"She was part of a group in California that restored historic buildings. She said it was so important to understand and appreciate the past so that we never forget what came before us, what made us who we are today." Despite the incredible view below me, I can't keep my eyes from the side of Luke's face as he speaks.

It's clear to see he loved his mother very much and I immediately think back to the reports I read on her death. Heart Disease I believe. As I study Luke's profile, it's easy to see that he is still haunted by the loss.

I can't help but feel like this is a side of Luke Scott few people see. It's strange really, seeing such a powerful, intimidating man let down his guard. There's something so beautiful about his vulnerability.

"Anyways." He shakes his head, pulling himself from the moment. "I guess I should go. If you need anything room service will take care of you." He seems to close down as quickly as he opened up, the sudden change leaving me with a feeling of whiplash.

"Will you be gone long?" I ask, hating that the question somehow seems desperate.

"I'm not sure." He answers, giving me a half smile. "Try to get some sleep." He backs slowly away from the window, eventually turning his back to me completely as he crosses the room towards the door.

"Luke." His name almost feels unfamiliar on my lips because I am so used to calling him Mr. Scott.

He turns back to face me just as he steps into the

hallway.

"Would it be possible for me to do a little exploring while we are here? I have a few places I would really like to see and I was hoping maybe I could squeeze in a couple of hours of sightseeing."

"I'm sure that can be arranged." He smiles. "Goodnight Allie." The use of the name leaves me with a bitter taste in my mouth but I swallow it down, nodding as he turns and disappears down the hall.

Hugging my arms around myself, I peer back out over the city, catching my own reflection in the window as I do. I stare at myself; study the lines of my face, the darkness of my eyes. I wish I recognized this girl. I wish I knew who she was but I don't. It may be my face that I see, but that doesn't change that the person staring back at me is nothing more than a stranger.

"So you think it went well?" I peer up at Luke as we make our way out onto the busy sidewalk, almost immediately colliding with an oncoming patron who shows very little remorse for nearly running me over.

"New Yorkers." He smiles, clearly catching the brief anger that flares in me over the man's reaction. "Don't worry, they aren't all like that." He glances back towards the direction of the man and then back down to me.

"Everyone seems so… stressed." I admit. "Like

they can't get where they are going fast enough." Coming from the West, it is a completely different feel than what I am used to.

"True, though I suppose most people that live here find that energizing. I love the hustle and bustle of the city. Mainly because it's so different but also because everything seems so alive. Not that L.A. doesn't have that too but it's just not the same. There's not a place on earth like New York." He grabs my elbow, steering me to the left past a long strip of massive stores.

"And to answer your question, yes, I think it went very well." He smiles down at me, before turning his attention forward again.

"So what happens now?" I ask, gently brushing into his arm as I try to avoid yet another patron who finds it necessary to walk in the center of the sidewalk.

I feel him tense at the contact and immediately correct the action.

"Sorry." I apologize, glancing up at the side of his face to see his forehead creased in concentration.

He remains silent for another long moment before finally answering my question.

"Tonight we will meet with Mr. Porter and his son to discuss finalizing Sco-Tech's offer. I'm hoping we did enough today to have them ready to discuss terms." He veers to the right, his hand going to the center of my back as he guides me in the same direction.

Heat immediately forms at the point of contact and begins slowly spreading through my limbs. I try not to let the feeling consume me but the task proves easier said than done. When he finally drops his hand an immense amount of disappointment immediately takes its place.

We continue the walk back towards the hotel in silence. It's clear Luke is in his head. I can sense the wheels turning every time I glance in his direction. I can't help but wonder what he's thinking about. What I wouldn't give to spend five minutes in that beautiful head of his poking around. If there is one thing I can say about Luke Scott, he sure knows how to keep people at arm's length.

It's confusing and infuriating and yet, completely understandable as well. I mean, I am his assistant after all. It's not like this is a personal trip. We are just here on business. He didn't invite me for any reason other than helping him close this deal.

But if that's true, why do I get this intense feeling every time his eyes meet mine? It's like he's two different people. Mr. Scott, my boss and then Luke, an incredibly attractive man that has me feeling things I know can't just be all me. There's something there, I know he feels it too. I don't know what he's done that justifies drawing that conclusion but I just know.

"Allie." I glance up at Luke, realizing immediately that he's talking to me and I, so lost in my own thoughts, completely missed whatever was said.

"Sorry, what?" I ask, feeling the heat flood my cheeks.

"I asked if you were hungry." He shakes his head on a smile, grabbing my forearm to pull me off to the side in front of a small little sandwich shop.

"This is one of my favorite places in the city." He gestures through the large window which puts the entire ten table restaurant on full display to the outside world.

"I could eat." I say, turning my attention back to him.

He gives me a wide childlike smile before pulling

the door open and ushering me inside.

I am immediately hit with the overwhelming smell of freshly baked bread. It's intoxicating and I find myself breathing in deeply as we approach the counter that sits along the back wall, a large menu displayed above it.

"This doesn't really seem like your style." I say the comment aloud without really meaning to.

"Just because my family has money doesn't mean I don't enjoy the same everyday treasures that other people do." He doesn't seem offended by the comment but I can't help but feel guilty for saying it.

"I know. I just…" I start but his laughter immediately ceases my words.

"It's okay Allie. I get it." He gives me a flashing smile before turning his attention to the young girl working behind the counter.

He rattles off his order without even glancing at the menu and then turns to me, gesturing for me to order. Quickly glancing back up at the menu, I settle for a turkey sandwich on rye and a cup of chicken tortilla soup.

After retrieving our order, Luke leads me to a small table in the corner, directly next to the large display window.

"So how did you find this place?" I ask, sliding into my seat as Luke takes the one directly across from me.

"When we were teenagers, Ryan and I would go out exploring the city while my father was here on business. We made it a point to never eat at the same place twice. After a couple of years and several trips to New York, we had dined in almost every corner of the city. But this was the one that always stood out to me. Now I always make sure to stop here anytime I am in the city." He says.

"Were you close, you and Ryan I mean?" I ask, taking a small bite of my sandwich.

I immediately see what Luke sees in this place as I go in for a second bite, the bread so good I swear I could eat it with nothing else.

"Well clearly you know we aren't that close anymore." He answers after swallowing his own bite, insinuating that I know Ryan far better than I actually do. I honestly have no idea of the inner workings of their relationship.

"I wasn't aware of that." I answer truthfully.

I know they have their differences and that Luke does not approve of a lot of the things Ryan does but it isn't until this very moment that I am learning that the tension runs deeper than that.

"Well you are now." He shrugs, knowing he can't take the statement back. "But to answer your question, not really. Ryan and I couldn't be more different and while there were and are things about Ryan that I love, at the end of the day we just don't see eye to eye."

"I'm sorry." My apology is sincere.

I had a sibling once and I can't imagine not loving him with my whole heart. It makes me sad that Luke has never experienced that type of bond with his brother, though it does make knowing what I have to do a little easier.

"Don't be." He brushes off the comment. "The Scott family has always been a family divided. Ryan has always been my father's son where I was my mothers."

"What happened to her?" I ask the question, wanting to see how far I can get him to open up.

Learning information about Luke is not the easiest of tasks. He is a very private person and for someone who is dying to know everything about him, it's hard not to pry.

I can tell by the way his shoulders go ridged and his eyes darken that this is not something he wants to talk about.

"Sorry, you don't have to answer that." I apologize, regretting asking.

"No, it's okay." He finally says after a few long moments of silence. "I don't usually talk to people about her." He turns his face to the side, looking out the window for a long moment before finally turning his gaze back to me. "She passed away when I was fourteen."

"I'm so sorry to hear that." My reply is soft.

While I already knew this fact, I can't contain the rush of emotion I feel knowing that I lost my mother at almost the same point in my life.

I wish I could tell him this fact; that I could tell him he's not alone and that I know what losing a parent at that age feels like but I can't. There is no way for me to reveal any of my past without risking revealing my true identity and as much as I want to, I know it's a risk I can't take.

"It was hard, especially given that after she was gone my father and Ryan both brushed her memory away like she had never existed." I can hear the emotion thick in his voice and can't control my urge to reach out and lay my hand on top of his.

He looks down the moment the contact is made and like a light switch, his entire demeanor changes.

"I'm sorry. I shouldn't be telling you this." He says, pulling his hand away.

I can't help the devastation that surges through me at his rejection. I want to comfort him. I want him to know he's not alone, but clearly that is not something he is willing to accept from me. I give him another apologetic look, not sure of any other way to react other than to just function as if nothing happened at all.

"I'm sorry, I shouldn't have asked about your personal life." I slide back into the mode of his assistant.

"What time are we meeting Mr. Porter for drinks again?" I ask, desperate to escape the awkward heaviness that seems to have settled around us.

"Seven." He answers stiffly, turning back to his food, prompting me to do the same.

"How far are we willing to go to acquire his company?" I ask, trying to push the previous conversation away.

"As far as we need to. It's vital that we continue to expand, especially with smaller companies that own a lot of the market in specific areas." He answers, letting the heaviness somewhat fall away as we move into a less sensitive subject.

We continue to make small talk throughout the remainder of lunch, mainly discussing work which Luke seems the most comfortable talking about. By the time we exit the restaurant a few minutes later, he seems back to himself for the most part, or at least that's what he's trying to make me believe.

The remainder of the walk back to the hotel is almost completely silent. I can't help but feel like I crossed a line I can't come back from by asking him about his mom. I've never really had someone to talk to about this kind of thing so I'm not really sure what the rules are here.

I am also in foreign territory when it comes to dealing with men, especially a man like Luke. One minute I feel like the electricity between us is going to cause the room to erupt in flames, the next I feel like the entire area has been doused in cold water. He's so back and forth, hot and cold, I find it exhausting and impossible to keep up.

But despite everything going on; my relationship with Ryan, Luke's inability to open up to me, my desperation to keep my real identity concealed, one thing remains true. I have never in my life felt the way Luke makes me feel. Deep down I think that scares me more than anything else.

Chapter Twelve

Luke

If there is one thing I can say about Allie Reynolds it's that she never ceases to surprise me. I knew bringing her along on this trip would be beneficial, even if there were selfish intentions involved in me asking her to come; like keeping her away from Ryan for example. But watching her now, seeing how easily she is able to manipulate Mr. Porter and his son Shane is unlike anything I have ever seen.

This woman is a natural. She knows exactly what to say, how to act, adding in just the right amount of flirting and flattery to have them eating out of the palm of her hand. What I thought may be a tough acquisition, Allie has actually made quite easy for me.

In less than two hours she has taken the two men's reservations about selling out to Sco-Tech and completely changed their way of thinking. The amount of detail she knows about our company is astonishing and I am quickly realizing that I severely underestimated just how brilliant she is.

I watch as she speaks, the way she leans across the table to truly engage her audience. When she drops her head back on a laugh and lays her hand lightly against

Shane's arm, my stomach tightens in an instant. I have to swallow down the sudden urge I feel to push his arm away from her touch. The thought leaves me a bit shaken but it's a feeling I can't deny.

Allie Reynolds, no matter how tempting, is off limits. Not only is she my assistant whom I need to maintain a professional relationship with but she is also seeing my brother, in some form or another. Though I know that will be over the moment he gets her into his bed so I'm not sure if that should even play a factor.

After less than three hours at Sachkets, the two gentleman rise from the table, Mr. Porter immediately turning to me.

"Well Mr. Scott, how about you meet me at the office tomorrow morning. Say ten o'clock?" He extends his hand to me the moment I rise to my feet. "We can go over the specifics and be done with this business then."

"I will be there." I agree, giving him a firm handshake before reaching out and shaking Shane's hand as well.

"Miss Reynolds." Mr. Porter turns to Allie. "I hope we meet again sometime my dear. I have a feeling you have a very promising career in this field." He winks, dropping a brief kiss to her hand.

"Thank you Mr. Porter." She smiles graciously, the familiar pink hue taking over her cheeks the moment her eyes flip to mine.

She immediately looks away, turning her attention to Shane who approaches her next.

"Here's my card." He leans in and kisses her cheek. "Call me the next time you're in New York." He waits until she takes the rectangular strip of paper before turning to join his father as they exit the lounge area of the bar.

"Did we do it?" Allie asks the moment to two men are out of ear shot. She hits me with an excited grin as she slides back onto her stool.

"You did it." I say, reclaiming my seat as well. "You were incredible tonight." I tell her truthfully, still a bit in awe of the woman sitting across from me.

"Me? I didn't do anything." She insists, her deep blush plain as day despite the dim lighting of the bar.

"Are you kidding me?" I give her a disbelieving look. "You made the entire deal happen. The only thing I did was have the sense to bring you along." I hold up two fingers to our waitress before she even reaches our table, signaling that we will take two more.

"Oh I probably shouldn't." Allie pulls my attention back to her when she realizes I am ordering more drinks. "I've already had more than I should."

"Nonsense, we're celebrating." I say, knowing that she has the right idea but not being able to walk out of this moment with her.

I just want to exist right here and now with her without considering all the reasons why I know I shouldn't.

"Are we now?" She laughs sweetly, the sound so fucking beautiful it takes everything I have not to reach across the table and pull her into my arms.

"We are." I nod to the waitress as she sits a new drink in front of each of us.

"Well if you insist." Her smile widens as she picks up her glass. "To your acquisition of Cyntech." She says, holding her glass up.

"To *our* acquisition of Cyntech." I correct her, lightly tapping my glass of scotch and water against the fruity pink concoction she has been drinking all night.

Chapter Thirteen

Samantha

"Luke Scott." I can't contain my laughter as Luke ushers me onto the elevator, squeezing my side as he does causing me to squeal out.

"She's ticklish." He nods, committing it to his memory, a devilish look in his eye.

"Don't you dare." I warn, squealing again when he makes a move towards me.

He immediately stops, holding his hands up on a laugh.

"I won't. I promise." The playfulness in his voice sounds through the enclosed space.

I give him one last warning glare and then turn my attention forward, trying to focus on keeping my balance as the elevator begins to climb. The trip up seems never ending and with each painfully slow floor we pass, the heavier I feel the tension inside the elevator grow.

After the Porters left the bar, Luke and I stayed and had several more drinks, celebrating what he said to be a closed deal. I can't remember a time where I have enjoyed myself so much. We laughed, we joked, but mostly we flirted. Exchanging heated glances for a good portion of the night, Luke didn't try to hide the fact that he wanted to touch me, using every excuse in the book to do just that.

You have something here. He said as he reached out and brushed his thumb gently against my bottom lip.

What happened? He had asked before trailing his fingertips lightly across the small, jagged scar on the back of my hand.

I knew early on that I needed to slow it down and I told myself the same thing with each moment that passed but I just couldn't bring myself to stop it. I wasn't ready to say goodnight to Luke. Hell, I'm still not.

My head spins slightly as the elevator jolts to a stop, causing what little balance I still have over my body to give and I sway slightly, reaching out to catch myself on Luke's arm as he steps up directly next to me.

"Whoa." He laughs, steadying me just as the elevator doors slide open.

"Thank you." I get out, too intoxicated to feel the embarrassment I am sure would normally follow nearly falling on my face.

"You okay?" He asks, making sure that once we step into the hallway I have completely regained my balance.

"I'm good." I immediately sense the closeness of his body, the heat radiating from him like that of a thousand suns.

Looking up hesitantly, the moment his eyes meet mine I know I'm in trouble. I don't even realize that his hand is settled on my hip until I feel his grip tighten. When I try to look away, he urges my face back up by placing his hand gently under my chin.

He gives me no choice but to meet his gaze and when I finally cave and do just that, the moment seems to slow down around me. Suddenly I am more coherent than ever before. I can feel every single emotion flowing through me. I can see the hesitation in his eyes which turns more to want with each second that passes. His hold is slipping; I can feel it as if it's my own. Or maybe it is my own as well.

It's like the hallway is closing in on us. I can feel the walls shifting, threatening to crush us in their path but Luke refuses to let me break the moment. He dips his face lower, tilting my face up further as he does, causing every nerve ending in my body to tingle in anticipation.

I hold my breath as my heart thumps rapidly inside my chest, so loud that all I can hear is the collision between it and my ribcage vibrating through my ears. Luke holds my gaze as he slowly moves closer, his hand holding my hip so tightly that I couldn't move even if I wanted to.

"Allie." He whispers my name, his face so close to mine that I can smell the scotch on his breath, feel the heat of it against my lips.

I stand frozen, not able to speak, not able to react. I'm seeing so clearly and yet my vision seems obscured at the same time. Moments pass and with them the tension mounts, pulling at my insides, stretching me to the point that I feel like at any moment I might simply just rip apart and be lost forever.

I know only seconds have passed but each one that does feels like an eternity. Like watching a movie in slow motion, I know the moment the decision is made. I see it in Luke's eyes, the resolution that shows through so clearly.

My breathing turn's rapid like I can't get air in fast enough and then it happens. At first it's soft, a light brush of his bottom lip against mine. But then all at once everything seems to snap and his mouth crashes down on mine like his very life depends on this kiss.

His hand on my hip moves to the small of my back as he pulls my body flush against his, his other hand wrapping in the back of my hair as he deepens the kiss. He tastes of alcohol and mint, the combination an intoxicating mixture causing my mind to fill with fog as his tongue works expertly against mine, pulling from me a want I didn't even know was possible.

Before I know it, my feet are being lifted from the ground. We bang into walls and struggle through the hotel door before I hear it slam behind us. I don't bother to open my eyes, I am too lost in Luke's touch, his scent, the way it feels to have his hands claw at my body like he has never wanted anything more than he wants me at this very moment.

I don't have time to think. I know that walking away now requires a strength I simply do not possess. I need this. I want this. I don't care what that means for tomorrow. All I know is that right here and now I've never wanted anything more.

I feel the soft mattress connect with my back before I even realize we've entered a bedroom. Luke's kiss become more feverish, more intense, but his touch remains gentle, hesitant, like he's afraid if he pushes too hard I might break.

I claw at his back as he settles over me, ripping at the fabric of his shirt until he finally breaks away from my lips long enough to allow me to pull it over his head. He settles back down over me, my hands immediately connecting with the smooth flesh of his back.

He grinds into me as his tongue works sweeps through my mouth, the feeling of him hard against me sending me into an almost animalist rage. All I want is to feel him, on me, inside of me, all of him. The alcohol makes me fearless and not afraid to take what I want, or maybe that's the effect Luke has on me. Either way I feel revived, like being brought back to life after years of barely living.

My hands go to the waistband of his pants and he props up enough to allow me to quickly unbuckle them before pushing them down over his hips. He kicks at the material until he is free of it; his lips moving from my mouth to my neck as he works open the buttons that run along the side of my black cocktail dress that holds the material closed.

When he finally manages to get the last button undone, he slides the material off my shoulder, his mouth immediately dipping lower. I can't contain the gasp that sounds from my throat as he does. His lips leave a trail of fire, lighting my skin with every inch they touch until my entire body feels ablaze.

Our bodies tangle together in one perfect formation. My hands roam his flesh, loving the ripple of muscle I feel beneath my palms. After all of our clothing has been removed and Luke is positioned above me, he pauses, looking down at me with a look that literally takes my breath away.

"You're so beautiful." His voice comes out shaky, his hand moving to gently trace the side of my face.

"Luke." I barely get out as a whisper.

I can feel the doubt slipping in, the fear winning

out, but just when I think it's about to pull me under Luke catches my gaze. Like so many times before, that one action holds me completely captive, making me face what is right in front of me and admit what it is that I truly want above all else.

Wrapping my hand around the back of his neck, I pull him back down to me, his lips immediately connecting with mine. I can feel the heaviness of his want, the thickness of him as he relaxes down on top of me. Lifting slightly, I urge him forward, gasping as he slowly begins sliding inside of me. I feel the incredible pull, the size of him stretching my petite body to the point that it's almost too much to take.

He stills once he has entered me fully, pulling back to make sure I am okay before he slowly begins moving inside of me. The feeling of being filled so completely by Luke is unlike anything I have ever experienced.

He commands my body like it is his own, reacting exactly as he tells it to, bringing me to a point of pleasure that I have never felt before. His movements become less controlled as my body adjusts to his size. Before long he is thrusting inside of me so forcefully that not one inch of my body can't feel him.

I feel it in my toes, in the tips of my fingers, the feeling spreads through me like blood rushing through my veins, leaving no inch of my body untouched by the pleasure until it's all I can do but fall apart below him.

Over and over again I crash, the feeling hitting me in waves as Luke continues to move inside of me. His hands grip my hips so tightly I swear I will bruise, his lips working against mine so passionately, I know they will be sore for days. Every part of my body feels the effects of his reign over me and not one part of me wants it to end.

Chapter Fourteen

Samantha

The severe ache pounding through my brain is enough to jolt me awake. I immediately cringe, the pain in my head so intense I can't seem to find the strength to even pull my eyes open. My mind swirls, trying to piece together a series of events that seem to flash through my memory like a slideshow being played on repeat until it stops and only one picture remains; Luke.

My eyes shoot open as I try to shake off the effects of the dream. But even as I am pulled completely into consciousness I can't rid myself of how real it all feels. Attempting to sit up, it isn't until I realize that I can't move that my entire body seizes.

Propping my head slightly, I squint through the darkness, trying to piece together exactly what is going on. It doesn't take long for the situation to sink in. Luke's naked body draped over mine is more than enough proof that what I thought was a dream wasn't a dream at all but a staggering reality.

My stomach twists violently forcing me to relax

back into the pillows and take a few deep breaths. I can't ever remember feeling so wrecked but wrecked is exactly what I am. Every inch of my body feels the effects from last night, from the alcohol still swimming in the pit of my stomach to the soreness in my limbs from the incredible night I spent in Luke's arms.

I turn my head towards Luke who is curled on his side, his arm and leg draped over me as he sleeps peacefully next to me. His face is partially illuminated by a small sliver of light seeping in through the cracked bathroom door which gives him an almost otherworldly glow. I have a feeling he would be beautiful in any light.

I can't resist the urge to reach out and run my hand down his face, my fingers catching on the slight stubble that runs along his jawline. This man is perfect; absolutely perfect. There is not one part of him that I don't find myself completely drawn to. From the way his touch brings me to life, to his crystal blue eyes that seem to look through my very soul.

When I push his hair away from his forehead, putting his face on full display, the reality of my situation seems to take hold. Dropping my hand away, the moment is broken by the panic that suddenly constricts my chest and makes it difficult to pull in enough air.

I grip the sheet below me and try to take a couple of deep breaths. How did I let this happen? The man laying next to me, the man who has completely changed my heart in the matter of one night has no idea who I really am.

The lines between Allie and Samantha are starting to become obscured by my quickly forming feelings for Luke. I thought I could do this, that I could just walk in and destroy someone else's life and not look back, but I was naïve to think there would be no additional casualties along the way.

Honestly, I don't think I really cared what happened to me at the end of all this. But Luke has changed everything. My priorities are starting to shift and I know that I am in too deep to approach this situation with a clear head.

Leaning up, I gently slide Luke's arm off of me and roll to the side as carefully as I can, trying my best not to wake him. When I manage to get his leg off of mine, he shifts slightly but does not wake.

Gathering my things, I quickly slip out of Luke's room and into my own, locking the door behind me. I have to get out of here. I have to remind myself what all this is for. Because no matter how much I want this with Luke, I know that it will never work.

I can't be Allie Reynolds forever. The girl he thinks I am, she doesn't exist. What will happen when all that's left is Samantha? Will he still want me then? I think knowing the answer to that question is just as devastating as the realization that I am going to have to let Luke go.

I am here for one reason and one reason only. I can't let myself throw in the towel when I have come so far. Ryan Scott will get what's coming to him. I have sacrificed everything to make sure that very thing happens.

Sliding on a pair of dark jeans and a long sleeve black shirt, I grab my boots from beside the bed before quietly exiting my bedroom. Grabbing a piece of paper and pen from the door side table, I scribble Luke a quick note, knowing that as my boss he at least needs to know what I'm doing.

Dropping it on the sofa table where I know he will see it, I slide on my coat and boots before quietly slipping out of the hotel room and heading downstairs. By the time I step out into the cool morning air, the sun has just broken the horizon giving the sky an almost orange color.

I snuggle deeper into my jacket and take off down the sidewalk, having no real idea where I am going. All I know is that I need to get away.

This is where I wish I had someone, anyone, that knew the real me and what I am actually doing here. Someone I could call that could talk me off the ledge and reassure me that I am doing the right thing. I have no friends, no family, no one that cares if I live or die. I am completely alone in this world, I think that's the scariest part of all of this and why I am so out of sorts over my night with Luke.

For the first time in a very long time I awoke feeling like there was more to life than this. That maybe love and friendship meant more than revenge. But then I remember what I've lost, that if not for Ryan Scott I wouldn't be alone in the first place.

With that thought alone I can feel my resolve slip back into place. Luke is a setback, a bump in the road I didn't see coming, but that doesn't mean that I have to get off the road completely. There is no future for the two of us, no matter what choice I make. My path to vengeance is all I have left now and I will cling to it until my plan is complete.

Chapter Fifteen

Luke

Visions of last night flood my sight the moment my eyes open. I take a deep breath, letting the memories seep in. Allie; the way she smelled, the way she tasted, the way she felt beneath me. I can't wipe away the immediate smile that crosses my face.

Sitting up, I realize immediately that I am alone. Even the disappointment of Allie not being here with me is not enough to shake the warm feeling last night has left me with. Throwing back the covers, I quickly climb out of bed, sliding on my boxer briefs before making my way out of the bedroom in search of Allie.

It doesn't take me long to realize the hotel room is empty. Not sure where she could have gone, I look around the room in search of my cell phone, not sure where it might have ended up in the chaos of last night.

Just as I turn to head back to the bedroom, I spot my phone on the table in the living room, a folded over piece of paper wedged underneath it. Pushing the phone to the side, I immediately open the paper to see Allie's beautiful cursive scrawled across the center.

> *Headed out to do some sightseeing.*
> *Be back later.*
> *-Allie*

Tossing the note back down, I grab my cellphone, preparing to call her. Before I can get her number dialed, the phone buzzes to life in my hand, a New York area code flashing across the screen.

"Mr. Scott." I recognize Shane Porter's voice immediately upon answering. "My father asked that I invite you to join us for breakfast." He continues without waiting for a reply.

The last thing I want to do is spend the day with the Porters, especially given that I am currently preoccupied with a certain beauty I had the pleasure of sharing my bed with last night. But alas, I know that business is business and there is no way I can decline.

"That sounds great. Where can I meet you?" I answer after a short pause.

"Baristas on Eighth. Can you make it by nine?" He asks, causing me to glance up at the decorative clock above the entry way; just after eight.

"Nine I can do." I reply.

"Perfect. We will see you then." He says.

"See you then." I reply, disconnecting the call.

Letting out a deep sigh, I decide to send Allie a quick text message before heading into the shower. I know it's foolish of me to get involved with my assistant, and then there's whatever is going on with her and Ryan to consider, but I cannot help the way this girl makes me feel.

She has completely fucking wrecked me in the absolute best way possible.

Chapter Sixteen

Samantha

> _Wish I could join you. I hope you have a good day._
> _I will be thinking of you._

I read Luke's message for the second time before snapping my phone shut and shoving it back into the pocket of my jeans. I know I am going to have to deal with this situation head on but right now it's not a thought I can stomach.

Crossing the main campus of NYU I look around at all the buildings, the layout, the scenery that Sean had described to me upon his arrival here all those years ago. Finding a nearby bench inside of Washington Square Park, I have a seat and watch as students cross through the area on their way to class.

Some are busy talking on their phones, some huddled in groups laughing and chatting, others have their nose so far in a book they barely look up to make sure they are going in the right direction.

I try to envision this life; what it must have felt like

for Sean, what it might have felt like for me had I been dealt a different hand in life. Would I have been like all these other young adults? Would I have attended college, had friends, boyfriends even?

The thought seems so foreign to me, probably because I have never truly considered that type of life for myself. I accepted early on that this was not in the cards for me.

I don't know how much time passes while I sit here watching the world go by. It seems like only minutes but when I finally decide to check my phone, I see that I have been here for well over an hour. Knowing I need to get a move on, I stand, stretching out my stiff legs.

Looking around the park one last time, I feel a sense of closeness to Sean that I have not felt in a very long time. Knowing that he was here once, that this was one of his favorite areas on campus, it makes me feel connected to him on a level I can't quite explain.

I flag a cab as soon as I reach the main road, asking the middle aged man to take me to the one place I dread going but know I need to see; the place where Sean died. I don't know exactly where it happened but I know what road it was on and that it was quite a ways outside of the city, so I ask the driver to just drive.

Miles and miles of road pass by us on our way out of the city; all the while my mind drifts to the night of Sean's death. These roads, these surroundings, were some of the last things he saw before his life was ripped away from him far too early.

I relive the moment we found out over and over, like a nightmare I can't escape. I can still hear my mother's screams as she collapsed on the floor, my father doing his best to comfort her as the police officer told her over and over again how sorry he was.

I remember being too young to truly grip the reality of the situation but being old enough to feel the pain of knowing I would never see my brother again. I know I'm not the only person in the world to ever lose a loved one. I know this is a pain that others feel everyday as well. I wish I could manage the pain, the rage, the devastation I feel for what happened to my family but I can't.

I guess that makes me weaker than most. Or maybe it means I'm stronger because I recognize the injustice and I seek to make it right. Either way, nothing will bring them back. I know that much. I think a part of me just hopes that somehow this will bring me the closure I am so desperate for.

Out of the corner of my eye I catch sight of a small wooden cross sticking up out of the ground just feet from the side of the road. It immediately pulls me from my thoughts and sends my voice echoing through the cab.

"Stop."

"Ma'am?" The driver seems confused considering we are on a bare strip of road without a thing in sight.

"Stop the car." I repeat myself, pushing open the back door before he even has a chance to pull the car to a complete halt.

Without a word I take off in a full sprint, backtracking the road we just traveled to the spot where I saw the cross. It doesn't take me long to catch sight of it again and I immediately dip off the road into the shallow ditch where it is located.

My heart is beating a hundred miles a minute when I finally reach it. Whether it's from the run or the knowledge of what this means, I'm not sure. I drop to the ground directly in front of the handmade cross, tears obstructing my vision as I do.

I blink rapidly trying to clear my line of sight, my tears flowing heavier when I finally make out what's written in black marker across the center of the cross; *Sean Allen Cole 1989-2008 Fly with the angels our friend.*

The sobs rake through my body when I realize what this means. Not only is this the very spot where my brother took his last breath, but this is where people who knew and loved Sean have chosen to memorialize him. The small bouquet of plastic flowers lying on the ground next to the cross is proof that not only did he have people here that cared for him, but he has people that still do.

I pull my knees to my chest and rock back and forth, my eyes darting from the sky to the cross, to the field directly in front of me where I know the accident happened. I am so lost in my own emotion, in the realization of where I am that I completely forget about the cab until the driver gently clears his throat behind me.

"Ma'am. Are you okay?" He asks hesitantly, staying a few feet back from where I am sitting.

"I'm fine." My voice comes out broken and riddled with emotion which I immediately try to reign in. "Can you give me just another couple of minutes?" I ask, not looking in the man's direction.

"Of course." He answers, walking away without another word.

I know that he's on my dollar but the fact that he shows no irritation or annoyance over the situation makes me extremely grateful. I'm sure it's not every day he has a crazy woman practically jump out of his moving car and take off sprinting down the road. Then again, this is New York. I'm sure he's seen crazier things now that I think about it.

I shake my head, turning my attention back to the cross in front of me. Words cannot express how much it means to me knowing that I am not the only person keeping Sean's memory alive. It brings me a comfort I wasn't even aware I needed.

It takes several more moments before I finally find enough composure to pull myself to my feet. Looking out over the field one last time, I can't help but feel like in this moment Sean is right here with me. I can feel it in the wind as it whips around my face, in the sudden peace that settles over my shoulders like an immense weight has been lifted.

Wiping away the last of my tears, I turn, making my way back to the cab which is pulled off the side of the road several feet in front of me. When I finally reach the car, I immediately climb into the backseat, asking the driver to take me back to the city.

If I was looking for confirmation that I am on the right path, I feel like I found it today. This is exactly what I needed; to remember what all this is for. For the brother I lost, the mother who was killed by her own grief, and the father who couldn't find the strength to go on.

By the time I finally make it back to the hotel room

it is already after seven in the evening. After the cab dropped me off outside of the building, I couldn't stomach facing Luke right away so I spent the next two hours roaming the area close to the hotel, stopping off at a hotdog stand to grab me a small bite to eat in the process.

Sliding my key card into the door, I hear the lock click before I push my way inside. The silence in the room immediately buzzes in my ears as I close the door behind me and drop my things on the floor in the foyer.

"Luke?" I call out hesitantly, not sure if he's here or not.

When I am answered only by further silence I push forward, collapsing on the stark white sofa that sits in the center of the living area. Pulling out my phone, I am shocked to see I have three text messages and a voicemail from Luke. I don't remember feeling my phone vibrate at any point beyond the first text message I received.

Sliding the lock screen, I check the text messages first.

Mr. Porter would like us to join him for dinner. Please try to be back by six.

Scrolling to the next message, my heart constricts slightly.

Are you going to make it for dinner? Please call me.

The time stamp shows this is the last communication from Luke. Guilt floods through me but I try to push past it. I have to find a way to separate my emotions. I am already in too deep, that much I know for sure.

Pressing the voicemail icon next, I hold my breath

the moment his smooth voice sounds in my ear.

"Allie it's Luke. I've been trying to reach you all afternoon. I am meeting Mr. Porter and Shane at *Dutchess* for dinner. In case you don't get this message in time I wrote the address down on the back of a business card and left it on the table in the entryway. I really hope that you are able to join us. I hope to see you there." His voice disappears as the line goes dead.

I know professionally I should join them. I should put on my game face, go get changed, and show up there ready to impress but I just can't find it in me to do so.

The day's events have me both mentally and physically exhausted, not to mention emotionally drained. I'm not sure I could smile at the current moment, let alone fake my way through an entire dinner. Besides, considering the time, they probably already have their entrees if not already finished eating.

Pulling up the text messages again, I offer nothing more than a simple reply to his invitation.

Sorry I wasn't able to join you. I got back a little late and did not see that you had called.
I'm not really feeling all that well and think I am just going to lie down for a while if that is okay.

His reply is almost instant.

I will wrap up here as soon as I can.
Is there anything I can bring you?

My heart picks up speed slightly, seeing how

quickly he jumps to my aid. Just another reason why walking away from Luke will prove to be one of the hardest things I have had to do to date. I have never had someone to worry about me or care about how I am feeling, it's both terrifying and gratifying.

> *Please don't rush. I will probably be asleep*
> *by the time you return.*

Staring at the messages illuminated on the screen, my heart breaks a little more with each second that passes. Each tick of the clock brings on a certain realization, one that reassures me that the life Luke makes me want, I can never have.

It's true that I barely know him. But it's also true that no one has ever made me feel the way he does. I can't explain it or even make sense of it but it's there, it's always there; this incredible pull that I can't seem to ignore.

I click off my phone, immediately forcing myself off of the couch. Crossing the space, I slip inside my room without even bothering to flip on the lights. While I may have fabricated my excuse slightly, the fact still remains that today has most definitely taken a toll on me.

Collapsing on top of the mattress, I don't even bother to pull the blankets down as I snuggle my face into the oversized bed pillow, a fresh set of tears immediately welling behind my tired eyes.

Chapter Seventeen

Samantha

I hear the main door snap closed, the sound instantly pulling me from my light sleep as I blink rapidly into the darkness. I hear Luke's light footsteps, one after another until they finally stop directly outside of my room.

Closing my eyes again, I try to keep my breathing even as I hear the bedroom door open slightly, a small sliver of light from the hallway shining directly on my face. It lasts only moments before the door latches closed and the light is gone.

Letting out a slow breath, I roll onto my back and look up at the ceiling. I wish there were some way out of the mess of a life I have created. I wish I could just let all of this go and for once just allow myself the chance at a normal existence. I wish a lot of things, most of which involve Luke.

I toss and turn for the next couple of hours, desperately wishing I could fall back to sleep. Luke finally settled in just a few short moments ago, the sounds of him moving through the hotel room dying off and leaving only an eerie silence surrounding me.

Pushing up in my bed, the moment my feet hit the floor they are crossing the room. I try to convince myself to turn around, to lie back down and just wait for sleep to come but I can't do it. The urge to see Luke, to touch him, comes on so fast and so strong that I have no choice but to follow it.

Before I can even process my body's movements, I am standing in front of Luke's bedroom door. I hold my hand up to knock, hesitating only a moment before I hear the sound of my fist connecting with the wood, the noise echoing through the silent hallway.

I hear nothing at first. No hint that Luke is awake, no movement from the room behind the door. Taking a step backwards, prepared to walk away, I immediately freeze when Luke suddenly appears in the doorway, his incredible body covered by nothing more than a tight pair of boxer briefs.

My eyes instantly drop to his bare torso, taking in the broad firmness of his chest before dipping lower to his sculpted stomach. I can feel the heat flood my cheeks as my eyes fall lower for a fraction of a second before finally finding his face.

"Allie?" My name is a question on his lips but he says it in a way like he's trying to convince himself that he's not dreaming, his eyes glazing over slightly the moment they take in my barely there attire; a tank top and boy short underwear.

Something about his reaction seems to break what little hold I have over myself, making me want to satisfy the sudden hunger that takes over his eyes. I step forward, wrapping my hand around the back of his neck before pulling down. He hesitates for only a moment before dipping down, his lips settling on mine. The softness of his kiss causes the sensation of needle pricks to spread across my skin.

I lose myself in my own desperation to feel something beyond my pain. I step forward causing Luke to step backwards into his room. He allows me to guide him two more steps before pulling me into his arms, kicking the door closed behind us.

The moment my feet hit the floor Luke pins me between his body and the back of the door, his kiss deepening as his hands slide the tank top from my shoulders, the giving material immediately sliding past my hips and pooling around my feet.

He sucks in a sharp breath as his hands roam my bare flesh, his touch becoming less controlled with each second that passes. I claw at his bare back, urging him forward, wanting to feel the pleasure I know only he can give me.

"I want to take my time." He pants, breaking away from my lips. "But if I don't feel you around me right now I'm going to fucking explode." The desperation in his voice sends my own need for him spiraling.

It's only moments before Luke has me panty-less and hoisted up, my legs locked around his waist as he slides slowly inside of me. He bites down on his lower lip like he's trying to control himself from just slamming into me.

Taking his face in my hands, I force him to look at me. "Don't hold back." My labored breathing makes my statement desperate and broken.

"I don't want to hurt you." He lays a gentle kiss to my lips before speaking against them. "I don't ever want to hurt you."

"You won't." I reassure him, knowing there is so much more to his statement but not able to process anything beyond the physical build.

He pulls back, the hesitation in his eyes fading as he finds something in my reaction that clearly gives him the reassurance he needs. Wrapping one arm around my waist and positioning the other one on the wall behind me, he thrusts upwards forcefully, causing me to cry out from the sudden intensity of his movement.

Tangling my hands in the back of his hair, I pull his lips back to mine as he begins moving inside of me. It's only moments before I feel like my body is going to split apart above him, each thrust harder than the last until every part of my body feels the burn from the fire he lights in me.

His mouth works skillfully against mine as he plunges inside of me over and over again, his tongue coaxing deep moans from me as he pulls every bit of pleasure from me that he can. There is not one part of my body that is not at his complete command.

He owns me. Right here and right now I am nothing but his; a body for him to control, a heart for him to claim. I am powerless to stop it. No matter how much I fight against it, I know I am no match for the feelings Luke brings to life inside of me.

"Look at me." His voice comes out a breathless rasp as his face hovers just inches from mine. "Look at me, Allie." He repeats when I hesitate to meet his gaze.

The moment I finally do, my entire body seizes, the look in his eyes sending my already failing grip on control completely spiraling. The burn turns to a scorch that starts at my feet and slowly works of my own heart, to the intense explosion that causes my entire body to tremble in Luke's arms.

"I can feel you." He whispers against my mouth seconds before his lips close down on mine.

His entire body goes ridged against me as he succumbs to his own pleasure, his legs shaking slightly beneath our combined weight as he rides out his release.

Resting his body against mine, he drops his face into the crook of my neck, stilling there for several moments, trying to calm his erratic breathing. I work slow circles across his back with my fingertips, loving the smoothness of his skin beneath my touch.

"I'm sorry." His voice finally breaks through the silence of the space, his statement confusing me.

"For what?" I ask, forcing his head up so that he has to look at me.

"I never meant for this to happen. Any of this. You're my assistant Allie. This is so wrong on so many levels." He starts, making no attempt to remove himself from my body.

"I just can't get you out of my fucking head." He continues, trailing a feather light touch across my collarbone. "How you feel under my touch, the way your breath hitches when I kiss you here." He drops his face, pressing his lips to the base of my neck invoking the exact reaction he predicted. "The way you feel around me." He moves slightly, the hardness of him still buried deep inside of me.

"Luke." My voice is weak and broken, the one word giving away exactly what his words are doing to me.

"This time I am going to take my time with you." There is so much promise to his statement, I feel the anticipation immediately begin to build inside of me as he backs me away from the wall and carries me towards the bed.

"I want to taste every inch of you." He breathes against my lips, dropping a brief kiss to them before depositing me gently onto the mattress. "I want you to feel what you do to me." He crawls up my body, his lips once again settling over mine as he kisses me more deeply, reigniting the flames still simmering deep within my body.

"Do you ever look in the mirror and feel like you have no idea who the person staring back at you is?" Luke's voice breaks through the darkness, his hand continuing to trail lightly up and down my back as I lay against his chest.

"Every day." I answer truthfully, caught off guard by the sudden change in conversation.

Just moments ago we were discussing our favorite foods and laughing over the fact that Luke can't pass a candy store without going inside to buy rock candy.

"Why do you ask?" I add on, not sure where this is coming from.

"I don't know. Sometimes I just look at my life, at my family, and I can't help but wonder how I fit into it all. Like the world I exist in wasn't made for me. Does that make sense?" His hand stops in the middle of my back for a brief moment before he begins working slow circles across the center with his fingertips, clearly lost in his thoughts.

"It does. It makes perfect sense actually." I can't help the sudden rush of emotion I feel having even a remotely genuine conversation with Luke.

I feel like so much of my life is falsified, it's refreshing to just utter the truth without a second thought.

"Like the sensation of being lost even when you are surrounded by people and know exactly where you are." I say aloud not actually even meaning to.

"Exactly." I can feel his smile against the top of my head as he lays a kiss to it. "I don't know, I just don't feel like I belong." He pauses. "At ScoTech, in Los Angeles, or hell even in the Scott family for that matter."

"Then why stay? Why work for your father?" I ask, curious why a man as clearly driven as Luke would accept anything less than what he truly wants.

"Honestly, I don't know." He laughs lightly, his chest vibrating against my cheek. "I guess partly because it was just expected of me."

"And the other part?" I ask.

"I don't know. A part of me truly loves it I guess." He admits, his voice dropping to almost a whisper. "I just wish I felt like it mattered more."

"Have you ever thought about what you would do? If you didn't work for your father I mean. What would you be?" I ask.

"I have never really given it that much thought honestly." He admits. "From the moment I was old enough to start learning the business that's what I did. My father used every opportunity he had to bring Ryan and me along with him on trips and business endeavors. Hell, I was sitting in a board room before I was even a freshman in high school. We were bred to take over this business. It's just part of me."

"Then why do you think you feel like the outsider?" I ask, genuinely curious.

"I'm just not like anyone in my family. Ryan and I couldn't be more different. It's almost like my father has never truly seen me for who I am. I have taken a backseat to Ryan since my mom died." His voice trails off.

"What was she like?" I ask the question hesitantly, knowing this is a sensitive subject.

"Like me." He sighs, his hand moving from my back to my hair, his fingers sliding through the wavy ends. "Only way prettier." He adds on a light laugh.

"Do you think maybe that's why your father favors your brother, because you are more like your mom and he is more like him?" I ask, still not having a full grasp on Nicholas Scott and just what kind of man he is.

"I think it hurts my father to be around me too much." He shifts beneath me, rolling to his side as he tucks me into his chest, my head resting on his arm. "Sometimes he will just look at me, really look at me, and I know it's because he sees her. I have her eyes, her dark hair. I am so much like her in so many ways. After she passed he moved to the city, he couldn't bear to stay at our Santa Monica beach house where he had lived with my mom, where Ryan and I spent most of our childhood, whereas I couldn't bear to leave it. I've lived there by myself ever since."

"Wait, so you've lived by yourself since…" I cut in.

"Since I was fourteen." He finishes my sentence. "Ryan chose to go to the city with my father. I liked it better that way. I mean, he hired a housekeeper to occupy the guest quarters and make sure I stayed out of trouble, didn't starve to death or burn the house down, and a driver to ensure I made it to school but other than that, he walked away from being my father the exact same week I lost my mother. I guess it was for the best." He shrugs, his body relaxing slightly against mine.

"I'm sorry." I say, not able to hold back the sadness I feel for the boy he used to be; the boy who lost his mom, and for all intents and purposes lost his father too, at such a crucial time in his life.

"It was a long time ago." He kisses my forehead.

"Even still, I'm sure a loss like that sticks with you." I say, choking back the emotion that thickens in my throat.

"I guess in a way it does. But a past shouldn't define a future. The cards were dealt and I played the hand the best I knew how. I think it worked out as it was meant to." His ability to just simply let go leaves me a bit in awe of the man lying next to me.

I wish I possessed that strength; to just let go and let the past be the past.

"And you don't resent your father for abandoning you the way he did?" I ask, not able to stop myself.

"No." He answers simply. "If anything I'm grateful. It's hard to say what the impact may have been had I remained with my father. I mean look at Ryan." He shakes his head.

"My examples were all set by my mother. She taught me the difference between right and wrong, what separates good people from bad, what truly matters in life. My mother was the best thing about my father. She was the only one who knew how to love him the way he needed and wasn't afraid to put him in his place. She forced him to prioritize family over work and insisted he be the father she felt we needed. Once she was gone he let his work consume him until he had nothing left. Nothing but his company and the one son that was blind enough to follow him into the same life. I love ScoTech don't get me wrong. It is my father's legacy and I will always strive to make him proud. But I also know there is more to life. My father doesn't feel the same way. Him and Ryan have that in common which is primarily why Ryan was selected to take on the company after my father retires. Like my father, my brother is driven by power. I know that running my father's company is all he's ever wanted and he's gone to great lengths to ensure he gets to do just that."

"What do you mean?" I try to keep my voice calm.

"Nothing." He shakes it off. "Let's not talk about my brother right now." He tenses slightly against me and I am suddenly reminded that in his mind I am somewhat dating Ryan.

"You're right, let's not." I agree, knowing that this is probably the last time I will ever get to be in Luke's arms.

Ryan has taken enough from me but I won't let him have this. This moment, this memory, the way I feel right now, is something he will never be able to touch. Snuggling deeper into Luke's embrace, I place my lips lightly to his chest and breathe in his scent as deeply as I can, trying to commit it to memory.

"Will you promise me something?" I ask, closing my eyes.

"Anything." I can hear the smile in his voice.

"Promise me that you won't ever lose who you are. No matter how lost you may feel or how much of an outsider you may be, don't ever conform to be like them. There are so many of *them* out there."

"I promise." He laughs lightly, nudging me. "Besides, you can always shove me in the right direction should I ever steer off course." His statement is enough to gut me right here on the spot.

I don't have the heart to tell him that this is all he will ever have from me, that when we return to California tomorrow it will be as if these last two days never existed, or that once my plan is complete he will never see me again. Not because it's what I want but because sometimes we have to sacrifice our own happiness for the sake of what is right.

Besides, when and if he learns the truth, he will probably never want to see me again so I guess ultimately I am doing him a favor. The sooner I end this, the less of an impact it will have on him.

I know my path.

I've made my choice.

Allie is already preparing to let Luke go, I just hope Samantha can handle the fallout of losing him.

Chapter Eighteen

Luke

I feel the warmth of Allie's body against mine before I even fully wake. Her sweet scent is the first thing I smell, her soft skin the first thing I feel; I think I could wake up every morning just like this. Peeling my eyes open, I turn to see Allie curled into my side, her dark blonde hair sprawled across her face obstructing my view.

Hesitantly reaching out, I brush the hair away from her face, sucking in a deep breath at how incredibly beautiful she looks right now, how at peace. There is something about this girl, something that makes me want to abandon everything I know and just be with her.

I know that I shouldn't, I know how wrong it is of me to take advantage of her vulnerability this way. I just can't stop myself. I have never craved a woman the way I crave this one. I have spent weeks trying to not think about her as anything other than my assistant but now, now there's no going back. Now that I have tasted her nothing will ever satisfy that thirst again, nothing but her.

She shifts slightly against me, her nose crinkling in the cutest fucking way as she snuggles deeper into my arms. It's the best fucking feeling in the world. But even as

I watch this peaceful angel sleep in my arms, this perfect beautiful girl that seems so innocent, I can't help but wonder what she's hiding behind those big chocolate eyes of hers.

I can sense it when she looks at me, the way she averts my gaze when the conversation turns to her. Something just doesn't quite add up here and yet I can't seem to put my finger on it. Trying not to put a damper on the morning, I quickly shake the thoughts away.

Allie once again shifts, this time rolling away from me, her petite body becoming even more tangled in the white linens that cover the bed. I can't resist the urge to reach out and trail my hand lightly down the smooth curve of her back, loving the way her skin seems to react to my touch even though she is lost to sleep.

Finally deciding I should get up, I reluctantly roll out of bed and quietly cross the space of the bedroom, slipping on a pair of boxers and a white t-shirt on my way out the door.

Deciding to order some breakfast, I have the coffee table in the living area lined with every single item on the hotel's breakfast menu by the time Allie stumbles out of the bedroom forty-five minutes later in an oversized t-shirt. She hits me with a crooked smile, pushing her disheveled hair away from her face as she slides down on the floor across from me and snags a piece of bacon, biting the tip off before saying even one word.

"I'm so hungry." She laughs, giving me an apologetic look after swallowing her bite of bacon.

"Good." I laugh, gesturing to all the food I ordered.

"What time did you wake up?" She seems surprised

to find me up so early given how late of a night we had.

"About an hour ago." I stack a couple of pancakes onto the plate in front of me. "You were sleeping so peacefully, I didn't want to disturb you."

"I can't remember the last time I slept so well." She admits, her statement immediately bringing a smile to my face.

"Perhaps when we get back to California I can show you what a good night's sleep really entails. You wouldn't believe how incredible it is falling asleep to the sound of the ocean waves crashing around you." I say, noticing instantly the way her expression falls as if I have just reminded her of something she didn't want to remember.

Setting down her half eaten bacon, she grabs a napkin and wipes her hand, refusing to meet my gaze.

"Allie?" I question, feeling like I just said something wrong.

After several long silent moments she finally meets my gaze, the sadness behind her eyes damn near knocking the wind right out of me.

"What is it?" I pry, needing to know what happened that changed her demeanor so quickly.

"We should probably talk about what happens when we return home." Her voice shakes as she speaks and it's clear to see she's very nervous.

"We don't have to rush things Allie. This doesn't have to change everything the moment we return." I reassure her. "There's no pressure here." I tack on, sensing maybe she feels like I have certain expectations.

"That's not it." She shakes her head, the sadness in her eyes only growing. "Look, these past two days have been probably the best in my life." She looks down, knotting her hands in front of her as she considers how to say whatever it is she plans to say next.

"It's just… Well, I can't…" She hesitates.

"You can't what?" I push, the anticipation reaching a boiling point inside of me.

"I can't continue to see you outside of a professional manner Luke." She hits me with an apologetic look. "I've really enjoyed our time here, more than you know, but you are my boss and then there's Ryan to consider." Her eyes widen slightly as she immediately takes in my reaction.

"Ryan?" I spit his name like its acid burning my tongue.

"You knew coming here that him and I were… Well, I'm not really sure what we are." She admits.

"I knew you two had seen each other a couple of times. I just kind of assumed after the last two nights that this would no longer be the case." I state, trying to keep my voice calm.

"I just… I don't know." She lets out a deep sigh, clearly trying to hold herself together.

"What don't you know Allie?" I cock my head slightly. "It's pretty simple really. Are you or are you not planning to continue to see Ryan when we return to California?"

Her bottom lip quivers slightly and I can see the answer in her eyes before she even utters a word. This realization sends me into a rage I didn't know this girl could make me feel. Pushing off the floor, I am already walking away by the time Allie manages to get up as well.

"Luke wait." She calls after me, causing me to spin around to face her just as I reach the hallway. "It's not that simple." She tries to explain.

"But it is that simple Allie. Either you're with me or you're not. Either you plan to go back to my brother after fucking me or you don't. What part is so hard for you?" I regret the tone I take with her but I can't reel it in. I can't hide how bad this fucking hurts.

I have spent my life competing with Ryan. Most things I don't care to let him win, but this… This is something else entirely.

"Luke, please. It's complicated." Allie pleads, the look on her face completely contradicting the way she claims to feel.

If I mean so little to her that she can just drop me for my brother then why are tears flowing down her face like she can't stomach the devastation she feels? I have to fight the urge I have to soothe her, to pull her into my arms and tell her that everything will be okay. She is the one doing this, not me.

"You know what; I will un-complicate it for you. This…" I gesture between the two of us. "This never happened. Going forward you are nothing more than my assistant and you will conduct yourself as such."

"Luke." Her voice calls to me once again but I wait until I reach the end of the hall where my bedroom is located before turning back to her.

"It's Mr. Scott." The statement seems to knock the wind out of her slightly.

When she sucks in a raged breath, it takes everything in me to hold my tone.

"I will arrange for a car to pick you up outside at two. Make sure you are ready to go by then Miss Reynolds." I step inside my room and slam the door shut.

Chapter Nineteen

Samantha

The car ride to the airport is one of the worst I have ever experienced. I have not seen Luke since this morning and every second I get closer to seeing him again my stomach knots tighter. I know I handled the situation this morning poorly. I shouldn't have just dropped it on him like that. I should have waited, maybe for the plane ride back when I knew he couldn't run from me, when he would have been forced to let me explain.

But isn't that exactly what he tried to do; give me a chance to explain? He tried and I couldn't do it. I couldn't come up with one good reason to tell him. I know that I have them but it's not like I can just tell him what my true intentions are. If I think he hates me now, I would hate to see his reaction to the truth of my situation.

When the car pulls up next to the small jet on the private air strip, it takes everything I have to peel myself out of the backseat. I let out a deep breath the moment I step outside and try to keep myself calm leading up to the very moment I step on the plane. My nerves ease slightly when I realize that Luke is not yet on board.

Taking a seat in the last of three rows of two seats, I slide in next to the window and immediately turn my attention outside. The spring day is gorgeous, sunny skies, birds chirping, and for a brief moment I mourn the loss that this city brings. First Sean and now Luke.

Though I refuse to compare Sean's death to my fallout with Luke, I also can't deny that both will have an impact that will most likely follow me for the rest of my life.

A man like Luke doesn't come along every day, especially for someone like me. The thought of never feeling his arms around me again is almost too much to stomach. Blinking away the quickly forming tears in my eyes, I take a few calming breaths, trying to pull myself together.

I turn my attention to the front of the plane when I hear someone step on board. The moment Luke comes into view, I suck in another sharp breath. Gone is the loving, laidback, boxer wearing Luke that I spent the last two days with. He's been replaced by a stoic, quiet man draped in a perfectly pressed business suit; his crystal eyes hidden behind a pair of aviator sunglasses.

He doesn't acknowledge my presence as he takes a seat at the front of the plane. It takes everything in me to stay in my seat. I want to run to him, tell him I was wrong, that it's not Ryan I want but him. And while all of that would be true, nothing else would be.

Luke deserves someone that can give themselves to him completely. I should have never put myself in this position, but when you come face to face with the very thing you want possibly more than anything else, it's not that simple to just walk away. When I'm with Luke it's like another person takes over.

It's like Allie disappears and the girl I really am, the one that deep down just wants to find more, comes blazing to the surface. I can't fight against my own heart; I never have been able to. But knowing the promise I made to myself and to my family has to trump everything else. Even the fact that my heart is literally breaking in two right now.

This isn't about me or even Luke. This is about Allie. The woman I created to do what Sam is not strong enough to do; face the person who ruined it all and finally make him pay.

As the plane takes flight, I say a silent goodbye to the girl I found in New York; the one I lost a long time ago, the one Luke brought back to life with just one touch. I tell her I'm sorry. I tell myself I'm sorry.

Swiping away the one tear that manages to escape my eye, I turn my attention from the sky to Luke sitting just a few short feet in front of me. I whisper a silent apology to him as well, knowing that I will never forgive myself for pulling him into all of this. I just hope one day I can make it right.

"Welcome back." I glance up to see Ryan leaning

casually against the doorframe of my office.

"Thanks." I give him the best smile I can muster, having forgotten during my time away just how deeply my hatred for this man runs.

"So I hear you worked wonders in New York." He pushes away from the door and crosses the space towards me before sliding down into one of the chairs across from me.

"I'm sorry?" I question, panic immediately rising in my throat.

Certainly, Luke wouldn't tell him…

Would he?

I had never considered that possibility until just now.

"Luke said you had the Porters eating out of the palm of your hand. According to him you are the only reason we were able to close the deal with Cyntech." His smile widens and I silently let out a slow breath of relief.

"Well I don't know that I would go that far." I shake my head. "Luke did all the work, I just showed up."

"Don't be modest. I've had the displeasure of speaking to that son of his directly. Not an easy crowd. Luke made a good call taking you along."

"Well thank you." I finally concede, not feeling up to going back and forth with him over something so minuscule.

"How about we head out early to celebrate?" He suggests, straightening the cuff of his suit jacket before meeting my gaze again.

"I really have so much here to catch up on." I answer truthfully, knowing that leaving early to go out with Ryan might just be the thing that costs me my job.

"How about after?" I throw out the suggestion, knowing I need to start moving things along with Ryan if I ever hope to gain any ground.

"Deal." He agrees, his smile widening. "Want me to pick you up at your place?" He asks, standing.

"How about I just meet you in the lobby? Say sixish."

"I love sixish." He gives me a devilish grin as he slowly backs out of my office, his eyes lingering on my face for a long moment before he finally disappears into the hallway.

"Ryan." Luke's voice pulls my attention back to the doorway just moments after I look away, his sudden presence startling me.

He nods to his passing brother, the look on his face showing his dislike for finding him leaving my office, before turning his attention back to me.

"Miss Reynolds." His expression turns hard as he steps inside my office and addresses me. It's clear to see this is the last place he wants to be.

This is the first time Luke has spoken a word to me since yesterday morning in New York.

"Yes?" I meet his gaze, not entirely sure how to address him.

"Do you have the breakdown for the Cyntech acquisition finalized? I need to present the final contracts at my three o'clock meeting." He says, his tone clipped and emotionless.

"I just finished it actually." I say, turning my attention to my computer. "I will email it over now." I say, glancing back up to Luke.

"Thank you Miss Reynolds." He answers, nodding once before disappearing from my office.

The entire interaction leaves a sick feeling in the pit of my stomach. I can't help but feel like he came in here simply because he saw Ryan leave and that thought makes my heart constrict slightly.

I don't want to hurt Luke, it's the last thing I want, but I know that trying not to hurt him at this point is all for not. I've already hurt him, the way he's treating me is clear indication of just how deeply.

I wish there were something I could do. I wish I could rewind the past seventy-two hours and do them all over again. But even I know there is not one choice I would have made differently. I won't regret the moments I spent with him. I can't. No matter how badly our time together ended, it was in those moments together that I felt more alive than I ever have.

How could I ever regret one second of it?

Chapter Twenty

Samantha

"This place is incredible." I say, looking around Ryan's massive downtown apartment complete with a spiral staircase that leads to a second story and a wall of windows offering an amazing view of Los Angeles.

The open floor plan is decorated very modern with clean lines, black detailing, and white furniture. It is exactly how I would expect someone like Ryan to live.

"You want a glass of wine?" Ryan asks, stepping into the large chef style kitchen that is separated from the living area only by a large wraparound bar.

"Please." I answer, crossing the space towards the windows.

The view immediately reminds me of the one from the hotel room I shared with Luke in New York. I push the thought away knowing that the last thing I need is to have Luke inside of my head right now.

"Here you go." Ryan steps up beside me, holding out a glass of wine to me before turning to face the window.

"Thank you." I say politely, taking a long drink. "And thank you for tonight. *Sepparos* was incredible." I try to find my comfort in the conversation, trying somewhat to convince myself that this situation isn't as unbearable as it feels at the current moment.

"It was my pleasure." He turns to face me pulling my gaze to him.

Giving me a smile that causes my stomach to twist viscously, I cover up my disgust with a smile of my own.

It took everything I had to agree to come back here with him and with each passing second I can feel the regret creeping in more and more making it near impossible to relax. I hold his gaze, hoping my feelings are hidden from the man staring back at me. If he picks up that something is off he certainly doesn't acknowledge it, or maybe he just doesn't care enough to.

I'm not stupid enough to believe this is anything beyond what he can get out of me but I need my way in, I need him to let his guard down. If this is the only way to make that happen then so be it. I just hope I have it in me to go through with it.

Reaching out Ryan takes my wine glass from my hand, turning to set both his and mine on the decorative table to his right before turning back towards me.

"I'm glad you agreed to come here tonight." His voice is low, seduction dripping from each word.

I know without a doubt that if I didn't know Ryan Scott for exactly who he is, I would be eating every bit of this up. He definitely knows how to lay on the charm when he wants to. Unfortunately, his attempts have the opposite effect on me, though I can't let him see this fact.

"Me too." I say, the words almost catching in my throat.

I try not to cringe when he reaches out and trails his

hand slowly up my bare arm, the contact causing a sick tingling sensation to spread across my skin. He takes another step towards me, eliminating almost any distance between our bodies as his hand wraps around the back of my neck.

"You look incredible in this." He breathes against my mouth, his hand trailing down the side of my red A-line dress.

I open my mouth to reply but before anything comes out, Ryan's lips close down on mine silencing my response. My entire body stiffens at the contact but I mentally force myself to relax into the kiss, knowing that I need to play this up as much as possible.

Unlike Luke's, Ryan's kisses are rough and demanding, his touch like acid against my skin. But that doesn't stop me from deepening the kiss. It doesn't stop me from slowly pushing his suit jacket from his shoulders or from unbuttoning his white collared shirt one painfully slow button at a time.

I slide my hands across his bare torso, my mind immediately flashing to how Luke's flesh felt beneath my fingertips. When I hear his voice, I swear it's my imagination, my mind playing into what my heart wants. But when I hear it again, my entire body freezes.

Ryan breaks the kiss just seconds before I can pull away, both of us turning towards the doorway where Luke is standing, a bottle of liquor in one hand, a stack of files tucked underneath his other arm, his attention solely on his brother.

"Oh shit Luke, I totally forgot you were coming over tonight." Ryan laughs it off, sliding his shirt back onto his shoulders.

My heart immediately drops into my stomach. This is the second time now Luke has shown up when I am with Ryan, both times catching us in a passionate embrace. It's like fate is playing some sort of sick joke on me.

"I can see why." Luke flicks his eyes to me for a brief moment, the hurt behind those crystal blues knocking the wind right out of me.

"Allie, forgive me. My brother and I have been given the unfortunate task of having to analyze every major competitor on the West coast in order to find our next group of profitable acquisitions." Ryan says, buttoning his shirt as he crosses the space towards Luke, grabbing the bottle of scotch from his hand the moment he reaches his brother.

"At least you didn't forget the liquor." Ryan laughs, setting the bottle down on the counter.

"No but apparently you forgot Dad wanted this done by noon tomorrow." Luke doesn't try to hide his annoyance from his brother.

"I guess I should probably get going, let you two get to work." I say, cutting into their conversation.

Grabbing my purse off of the couch, I make my way towards the door, eager to escape the confines of the apartment.

"You could always stay and help us. I'm sure we could find a use for you." Ryan slides in front of me, blocking my ability to exit easily, his hand immediately locking around my waist.

"I think I would just be in the way more than anything." I say, trying again not to cringe when Ryan leans in and lays a kiss to my bottom lip.

'Nonsense." He shakes his head. "You'd probably be an asset if anything. Tell her Luke." Ryan is purposely baiting his brother, this much couldn't be clearer.

"I think Miss Reynolds has probably worked enough today." Luke answers dryly, avoiding my gaze.

"I really should go." I insist to Ryan, placing my hand on his chest.

"We will continue later?" He asks, his voice hushed.

I give him a weak smile and a nod, managing to escape his grasp without any further incident. I can't help but look in Luke's direction one last time before reaching the door. I don't expect the curious look I see plastered on his face when our eyes finally meet but that one look leaves me feeling a bit exposed.

"Miss Reynolds." Luke gives me a slow nod.

"Luke." I nod, disregarding his previous request that I address him as Mr. Scott.

This causes his lip to twitch slightly and for a moment I almost think I see a hint of a smile on his mouth.

"I'll call you later." Ryan pulls my attention back to him as he pulls the door open for me.

"Okay." I agree, allowing him to kiss me one more time before quickly exiting the apartment.

I exit the building, practically sprinting out of the lobby, doubling over the moment I reach the sidewalk outside. Placing my hands on my knees, I take a few deep breaths trying to calm the sudden urge to vomit that is slowly creeping up my throat.

Why did Luke have to show up?

Why of all people did he have to be the one to walk in and find me with his brother like that?

My mind swirls as it tries to process the events of the last five minutes.

When he first arrived he seemed furious. Even

though he made no attempt to vocalize it, I could still feel it pouring out of him. But as I was leaving I could physically feel the shift in his demeanor. What did he see that caused such a drastic change in the matter of seconds?

I try to replay the moment over and over again. He watched Ryan kiss me; I can't think of anything else. What was it in that interaction that he saw? Paranoia takes a forefront in my mind as I try to rationalize with myself that there is no way he could know anything.

Only what if he does?

Luke saw me in a way that no one else has ever seen me. Sure, I was still pretending to be Allie with him but he saw more Sam than Allie, he just didn't know there was a difference.

What if now he does?

I can feel my perfectly laid out plan slowly slipping out of control and this realization does more than just scare me, it downright terrifies me. I never considered the possibility that this wouldn't work, I only knew it had to.

But I never anticipated Luke. Never in my wildest dreams did I think that everything would hinge on my ability to not fall in love with a Scott. And now that I am, I feel everything slipping through my fingers leaving me grasping to hold the last remaining pieces in place.

Chapter Twenty-one

Samantha

I take a deep breath before reaching out to rap my knuckles against Luke's office door. Letting it out slowly, I wait until I hear him say "Come in" before pushing my way inside, shifting the stack of files tucked under my arm in an attempt to balance them all on one side.

Luke barely glances up when he sees me enter, keeping his attention focused on the material in front of him, he gestures to the corner of his desk, indicating where I can put the files.

"Is there anything else you need?" I ask, setting the stack of folders down on the dark wood.

"That will be all." His response is short as he continues to flip through the file directly in front of him, not once glancing up at me.

"Luke." I start but the minute his name leaves my lips he hits me with a warning glare, the look in his eyes telling me not to push my luck.

"You will address me as Mr. Scott, Miss Reynolds."

His voice is like steel, hard and unwavering.

"Or what?" I challenge, letting my emotions get the better of me.

"I'm sorry?" He tilts his head to the side and gives me questioning look.

"Drop the professional crap, we both know we are far past formalities at this point." I say, trying to rein in my frustration, knowing this is my fault not his.

"What do you want?" He sighs, pushing back in his chair as he runs a hand through his hair, clearly agitated.

"I want to apologize for last night. I never… I'm sorry you had to see that." I say, sliding down onto the edge of one of the chairs that sits on the opposite side of Luke's desk.

"I wish I could explain." I try to continue but he immediately cuts me off.

"I don't want an explanation unless you plan to tell me what exactly it is that you're after." He says, narrowing his gaze.

"I'm sorry?" I question, taken aback by his statement.

"You heard me." He leans forward, resting his elbows against the desk in front of him.

"I'm not after anything." I answer, the knot in my throat growing tighter.

"Bullshit." He spits.

"Why would you think I'm after something?" I ask, doing my best to come across as surprised and innocent when in fact I am neither of these things.

"Because Allie, it makes no sense. You spend two amazing nights in my bed, and don't say it meant nothing to you because I know that it did, but then the moment we return home you run back to Ryan like you can't get there fast enough. I wonder what he would think about our time in New York." There is a threatening nature about his statement causing fear to spread through every inch of my body.

"Luke…" I start, but once again he cuts me off.

"Don't say another word unless you intend for it to be the truth. I'm not stupid Allie. I see the way you look at me and I've seen the way you look at Ryan. You don't have feelings for him. You're using him, I just can't figure out why." He studies me for a long moment, anticipating my next words.

When my response doesn't come immediately, he continues.

"Tell me what your play is?"

"I don't know what you're talking about." I insist, knowing that if I expose myself to Luke now, everything I have worked for will be for not.

"Don't lie to me." His crisp tone bounces off the walls around us, the sound causing me to jump slightly, startled by the sudden violence in his voice.

"I'm not lying to you Luke. Ryan and I have a connection. We hit it off early on. Yes, the situation with you did complicate things but I am doing my best to get on with my life. Don't get me wrong, the time I spent with you was amazing but it was also a mistake. You are my boss, I never should have crossed that line with you and I am so very sorry that I did."

"You're sorry? You act like I wasn't there, like I didn't see you, like I didn't feel your reaction to me. You can sit there and play stupid all you want, I'm not buying it. Ryan is not the one you want, I am." He pushes away from his desk, standing.

"Luke, I don't know what you're expecting me to say here." I try to fight the quiver in my voice as he crosses the space towards me.

"I want the truth." He steps directly in front of where I am sitting.

Leaning forward, he places his hands on the arm rests on either side of me and leans forward, his face coming to a stop just inches from mine.

"I'm telling you the truth." I get out weakly, my hands shaking in my lap.

"Tell me the truth Allie." He repeats.

"Who do you really want; Ryan or me?" He leans closer, his lips hovering so closely to mine I can almost taste him.

"Luke, please." I plead.

"Tell me." His tone is harsh. "Do you want Ryan? The man you can't even look at without cringing. Or do you want me? Tell me you don't feel it too. This…" He trails his bottom lip lightly against mine, my entire body erupting at the contact.

"See." He points out. "Look at how you react to my touch. You want this as badly as I do. Now stop fucking lying to me."

"Why are you doing this?" My labored breathing causes my words to come out airy and broken.

"Why am *I* doing this?" He seems amused by the question. "I am not doing anything Allie. You are. You're lying to me and I want to know why."

"I'm not lying to you." I continue to insist.

"Then make your choice. Because if you say his name, we are done." He warns.

"I've already made my choice." I remind him, fighting back the well of emotion that comes boiling to the surface.

"Then say it." He pulls back slightly so that he could look into my eyes.

"Say it Allie. Say his name."

It takes everything I have to answer. The words catch in my throat and I have to physically choke them out.

"Ryan." My voice breaks on the word.

He leans forward slowly like he is going to kiss me but then stops just inches from my lips.

"Get out." He growls, pushing away from me and crossing the space towards the door before I have even had time to react.

"Get. The. Fuck. Out." He says each word slowly, ripping open his office door.

I try to fight back the well of tears behind my eyes, knowing that I've made my choice, revenge over love, and now I have to commit to that choice. Pushing out of the chair, I quickly make my way towards the door, avoiding Luke's gaze the whole way.

Just as I step over the threshold his hand darts out and grabs my forearm, halting my movements. Leaning his face down just inches from my ear, when he speaks a chill runs through my entire body.

"I know you are up to something. Whatever it is, I hope it's worth it." He lets go of my arm and steps back, allowing me to exit his office without another word.

I jump slightly when the door slams shut behind me. It takes everything I have to make it into my office without collapsing. Shutting myself inside, I lock the door and immediately turn, sliding down the hard wood to the floor.

Pulling my knees up to my chest, I drop my head down and try to calm the tremors that are running through my body. I have never been so terrified and yet, so emotionally devastated at the same time. It's such a chilling combination. Knowing that not only is Luke onto me but that I also just sealed my fate where he is concerned.

I can't help but wonder how much time I have left. How much time do I have before Ryan starts getting suspicious? Better question; how much time do I have before Luke tells Ryan about our time in New York?

One thing is clear; time is not on my side anymore.

I need to make something happen and I need to do it now.

Pulling to my feet, I quickly cross the space of my office, picking up the phone from the top of my desk before turning my attention to the key pad. With shaky fingers I enter his extension, waiting for his voice to come on the line.

"Ryan Scott." He answers, already knowing it's me based on the fact that all the office phones have caller identification.

"Ryan, it's Allie. I was wondering if we could get together tonight." I say, hearing the smile in his voice the moment he replies.

"I would like nothing more." He says.

"Perfect. I will meet you at your place, say eight?" I suggest.

"Eight sounds perfect." His reply is instant.

"I'll see you then."

"I look forward to it." His smooth response comes just moments before the line goes dead.

Chapter Twenty-two

Samantha

"Are you sure about this?" My next door neighbor Penny asks, clearly unsure as to why I would be here asking for a drug to render someone unconscious when we have spoken only once before and that's when I paid her to pretend to be my internship boss.

It's no secret that Penny does not run with the best crowd and I know for a fact that her boyfriend Carson deals drugs out of her apartment. In the few months I have been here I have seen more than a little bit of shadiness going on across the hall, which is why I knew exactly where to come when I decided what had to be done.

"I'm sure." I say, crossing my arms in front of my chest as I watch her boyfriend Carson pace the living room, his phone attached to his ear.

"Why do you need this again?" She asks, eyeing me curiously. "You don't look like a user."

"It's not for me." I state dryly.

"Obviously." She rolls her eyes, taking a long drag off of her cigarette before smashing it down into the ashtray in front of her.

"What are you planning?" She questions, like there is any way in hell I am going to tell her.

"Let's just say the less you know the better." I reply, causing her to nod her greasy blonde haired head in approval.

"I can respect that." She says, pulling out yet another cigarette and lighting it, taking a long drag, and then exhaling before continuing.

"You don't really fit in here." She observes, gesturing to my business attire, having stopped here directly after work.

"I'm not from here." I shrug, turning my attention to Carson the moment he disconnects the call he's on.

"I'll have it to you in two hours." He holds out his hand, taking the three hundred dollars from my fingers the moment I extend it to him.

"Thank you." I stand, eager to escape my current company.

Carson gives me a curious look, his shaved head and neck tattoo making him look a lot more intimidating than he probably would otherwise. Either way I don't know these people and honestly I don't want anything to do with them other than getting what I need.

"You sure about this?" He asks just as I turn to leave.

"About what?" I ask, turning back to face him.

"Pretty little thing like you, you sure you want to get mixed up in whatever you're planning?" He asks, taking the cigarette out of Penny's hand before sucking a long drag from it.

"Just make sure you have it to me by seven." I say, choosing to ignore his comment as I quickly exit the apartment without a backwards glance.

I arrive at Ryan's just minutes before eight o'clock. Dressed in a skin tight black tube dress and killer heels, the moment he answers the door it's clear to see the lust in his eyes. If I have done one thing right, it's keeping Ryan hanging on for so long. I think the anticipation of having me has somewhat clouded his judgment which is definitely working in my favor at the moment.

I waste no time stepping inside, laying a passionate kiss on his lips the moment the door latches closed behind me. He reciprocates, deepening the kiss as his hands grasp my hips pulling my body into his so that I can instantly feel the hardness of him against my stomach.

"Let's have a drink." I break away from his mouth on a pant.

"Okay." He licks his lips, not able to keep his eyes off of my body as I shimmy my way into the kitchen to make us each a drink.

"Where do you keep your scotch?" I ask after retrieving two crystal glasses from the cabinet.

"There's a bottle on the back counter." He says, making his way into the living room where he proceeds to turn on some music; a light jazzy sound immediately flooding from the speakers that are wired throughout the entire apartment.

Retrieving the scotch, I pour each of us a quarter of a glass before adding a couple of ice cubes to chill the drink. Making sure Ryan is not looking, the moment I see that he is messing with the fireplace, his back to me, I pull the small pill from my bust and break apart the capsule, pouring the contents into Ryan's glass before swirling the liquid with my finger to make sure there is no trace of the substance.

Jumping slightly when Ryan appears behind me, grinding himself into my backside, I quickly turn and push the drink into his hand.

"To us." I say, holding up my own glass.

"To us." He agrees, clinking his glass lightly with mine before draining the contents.

I do the same, even though I hate scotch.

Taking his empty glass from his hand, I turn and set both his and mine on the kitchen island before turning back towards him. Kicking off my heels, I immediately reach for him, my hands going into his hair as I pull him down into another passionate kiss.

According to the research I have done on Sinfixphor, I only have about ten minutes before his consciousness starts to fade and his memory will be compromised so I have to act fast.

Backing him towards the living room, the moment we reach the couch he collapses onto it pulling me down with him. Straddling his lap, I allow him to slide the material of my dress down, revealing my black lace bra. He sucks in a sharp breath, his mouth immediately finding my skin as he nips and sucks at my flesh.

I egg him on, moan and grind myself down onto his crotch, trying to make my performance as believable as possible. Grabbing me by the backside, Ryan lifts me up and deposits me down onto the couch, his body coming down on mine within seconds.

His hands are everywhere, my chest, my thighs and then even more. It takes everything I have to allow him to push the material of my panties aside. Everything in me is telling me to stop this, to stop him, but I know I can't.

I close my eyes, preparing for the moment that his fingers will enter me but that moment never comes. Ryan mutters something causing my eyes to flip to his face.

"Ryan?" I question, knowing the drug I put in his drink must be starting to take effect.

His body relaxes down on mine, his full weight making it nearly impossible to breath beneath him.

"Ryan?" I question again, feeling his body go completely limp above me.

Knowing it's now or never, I immediately begin trying to push Ryan off of me. When I had planned this out I had not anticipated that when he passed out it would be on top of me. Then again, I didn't really plan this out for long.

Having realized that sleeping with him was not something I thought I could stomach, especially given how I felt last night when I thought just that was about to happen, I immediately started looking into alternatives, which is how I came up with the plan to drug him.

It took less than two hours for Carson to come through and that's when this plan truly came to life. So basically I have had about two hours to map this out in my head which given what I am doing is not that much plan time. I am truly winging it here.

Finally managing to slide out from under Ryan, it takes me another few moments to get him rolled over onto his back. Working open the front of his pants, I manage to get the material over his hips before sliding them down his legs and depositing them on the floor.

According to Carson he should be out for at least two hours but I still know I need to work quickly. I can't risk the drug wearing off early and being discovered.

I move to his boxers next, knowing the scene has to be believable. I need Ryan to wake up thinking that what we started before he passed out actually came to fruition. I need him to believe that we slept together even if the details will be foggy.

Sliding his boxers off feels like a violation somehow and I can't help but look away as I do it, not able to take advantage of another person in this manner, even if it is Ryan Scott. Next is his shirt, which proves more difficult to remove than I anticipated.

By the time I finally have him naked I am completely exhausted. I don't think I realized how difficult it would be to maneuver someone of Ryan's size given how little I am myself.

Now to set the scene…

Fixing my dress, I quickly slide out of my panties, tucking the material in the couch cushion next to Ryan, making sure they are positioned in a way that he will find them and assume that I couldn't locate them before I slipped off after he fell asleep.

Crossing the space to the kitchen, I grab the bottle of scotch, rinsing his cup out with it to ensure no traces of the drug are left behind. I then leave a small amount in the bottom of one cup and leave the other empty, draining the remainder of the bottle into the sink wanting Ryan to believe we drank the entire thing.

Crossing back to where Ryan is passed out on the couch, I set down the two glasses on the coffee table and then tip the empty scotch bottle on its side. Grabbing Ryan's shirt from the floor, I toss it a few feet from the couch before kicking his pants off to the side, making it appear as though the clothing had been removed and thrown haphazardly in the heat of the moment.

Taking a deep breath I look around the space. Once I am certain that everything looks in place, I set off up the stairs, determined to search every inch of this apartment if that's what it takes. Ryan Scott is a shady man and therefore is bound to have hidden demons. I intend to find them and expose him once and for all for the man he truly is.

I start in his bedroom, knowing this is typically where most people store personal items. Unfortunately for me, it becomes apparently clear that Ryan is not a man that keeps many things lying around. I search his entire bedroom and mange to find not one thing.

Moving onto the guest rooms, I search each one top to bottom finding very little of anything outside of bedding and room décor. Fearing I made a huge mistake, I decide to check the last room on the second floor before I call it.

Because the second floor hall is open to the main floor below, it allows me to verify that Ryan is still out on my way to the last room. When I reach the door I am surprised to find it locked. Fiddling with the nob, I end up using a pin from my hair to pick the lock open. Lucky for me it is nothing but a standard bedroom door lock and proves rather easy to open.

Pushing my way inside, I close the door quietly behind me before flipping on the light. The moment I turn I realize that this must be Ryan's home office. There is a small conference table in the center of the large room, a dark mahogany desk sitting along the back wall, and shelf after shelf filled with manila folders, all of which appear to have several documents in each of them.

I know immediately that it will take me hours to sift through all the information in this room so I opt to check places that he is more likely to hide stuff he doesn't want someone finding. I search through a black filing cabinet next to the desk first, finding mainly ScoTech client documents and other various work related items.

Turning my attention to his desk, I search through each drawer, feeling my frustration grow with each one I open and close empty handed. Sliding down onto the floor, I check the last drawer on the bottom before I finally decide that this is useless. There's nothing here.

But just as I start to get up, I catch sight of something out of the corner of my eye and immediately turn my attention to underneath the desk. Upon closer inspection I find that there is a secret compartment under the main slab of wood that is locked.

Remembering the small ring of keys I found in the top drawer of the desk, I immediately retrieve them, sliding back under the desk. There are at least twenty keys on the ring and it's very possible that none of them will open this drawer but I am determined to try every last one just in case.

When I slide the second to last key into the key hole and turn, I can't contain my excitement when the lock clicks free. Sliding the drawer, it detaches completely from the desk so that I am able to set it in my lap in order to search through the contents.

There isn't much inside; a monogramed money clip, a handful of pictures, and a printout of ScoTech's 2014 earnings which appear to have been in the hundred millions. Flipping through the photographs, each one of Ryan with different a woman, I come to stop on the only picture that does not contain Ryan's face.

It's of a young girl probably around the same age as I am now. She has blonde hair and striking green eyes, a large smile displayed across her pretty face. Something about her is so familiar and yet, I can't pinpoint where I may have seen her before.

Setting her picture to the side, I quickly realize there is another compartment underneath. Sliding my nail along the edge, I am able to pry the top section off revealing the hidden section below.

The second compartment is completely empty with the exception of one item; a single flash drive. Having no idea what the flash drive may contain, I know that Ryan would not have gone through the trouble of hiding it if it didn't have something on it he didn't want anyone to find.

Reassembling the drawer, I quickly slide it back into the track underneath the desk, locking it before dropping the keys back into the top drawer. I have no idea if what I have found amounts to anything but I know that my time is running out. If I plan to get out of here before Ryan comes to then I need to get a move on.

Accepting that this is all I can get for now, I quickly make sure everything is back in place before shutting off the light and backing out of the office, locking the door on my way out.

Heading back downstairs as quietly as possible, I breathe out a deep sigh of relief when I see Ryan is still passed out on the couch, his breathing even and deep.

Crossing to the kitchen, I locate a piece of paper

and a pen from one of the drawers. Scribbling a quick note…

Thank you for an incredible night.
I'll call you later.
XO
-Allie

Leaving the paper on the kitchen island, I quickly retrieve my heels and my purse before slipping out into the hallway, the picture of the mystery girl and the flash drive still clutched firmly in my hand.

Chapter Twenty-three

Samantha

Finally safe in the confines of my own apartment, I collapse down in the middle of my mattress and pull my laptop into my lap, sliding the flash drive into the port. Opening the file, I scan each document, trying to decipher exactly what each one is.

Starting with the picture files, I open the first, immediately recognizing the young girl whose photo I took from Ryan's when I retrieved the flash drive. Clicking to the next photo, it's a picture of the same girl and a much younger looking Ryan studying in what looks like a park, clearly taken by another party.

Flipping to the next not expecting to find anything much different than the first two, I immediately freeze when the smiling face of my brother comes into view, next to him the same blonde girl.

Suddenly the realization hits me. I've seen this picture before. That is why this girl looks so familiar because I _have_ seen her before just not in a way that I could remember upon first sight.

     This is one of the pictures that were with Sean's belongings that my parent's packed up when they cleared out his room in New York. I remember it so clearly because I remember looking at the picture and thinking how happy he seemed, which in turn made his death even harder to accept.

     Why would Ryan have this?

     Clicking on the first file, it is an old scan of a college article written by a student that was published in their version of a newspaper. The article is dated April 8, 2008 which is exactly one month prior to the accident that took Sean's life.

     Reading on, I can't help the tears that immediately blur my vision at the article's content. The bright smiling young girl from the previous pictures now the center of a tragic piece.

Drug Overdose Rocks College Campus

Sarah Hassell, 19, was found dead of an overdose in her dorm room on campus early Monday morning. According to reports, Hassell had spent the evening with friends and returned to her dorm sometime after one o'clock in the morning. Her roommate found her non responsive around nine a.m. the next day, immediately calling 911. Paramedics pronounced her dead upon arrival. Friends and classmates are shocked by the discovery, many claiming that they had no knowledge of Hassell's drug use. Autopsy reports confirmed that a lethal dose of heroin was found in Hassell's system. This is one of many drug related deaths this year among college students.

I click off of the article, the content making me

extremely anxious to see what else the drive contains. The next file is even more curious than the first; Sarah Hassell's official autopsy report. Why would Ryan have this? Why would he need it for that matter?

I immediately know in my gut that Ryan is somehow related to this situation, I just don't know how yet.

Clicking on the next file, I have to blink several times before I finally realize exactly what I am looking at. It's the official police report from the accident that killed Sean. According to the report, Ryan was given a breathalyzer on scene and blew four times the legal driving limit.

Listed in the report is one casualty; a white male, late teens, who was pronounced dead on arrival. I swallow down the hard lump in my throat and open the next document. Like with Sarah, Ryan has a copy of Sean's official autopsy report.

His official cause of death was *Traumatic Aortic Disruption* which I know means his heart was damaged in the accident. That much my parents did tell me.

Something about seeing it here in print makes it so much more real. I know that sounds odd given that Sean died eight years ago. But seeing it like this, right in front of me, makes it seem so final. It's hard to think about the fact that this happened to someone I loved so much, someone I still love.

I quickly move onto the next file, eager to escape the mental picture that has taken over. The next document is Ryan's sentencing paperwork from the trial; the trial where the judge was paid off by his father to throw out the evidence of Ryan's intoxication.

I've studied the public documents on this case with a microscope but unfortunately for me, men like Nicholas Scott are very good at covering their tracks and I was never able to find anything concrete that tied him and the judge together.

Closing out of the file, I can't seem to connect the dots completely.

Why would Ryan keep a flash drive with documents from Sarah's overdose and Sean's accident tucked away in a secret compartment in his office?

Why are there pictures of both Sarah and Sean together?

How well did the two know each other and how is Ryan tied into the whole situation?

I can't help but get the feeling like somehow the two are connected but it makes very little sense how they could be.

Could there be more to Sarah's death?

Could Sean have somehow been involved?

Questions fly through my head faster than I can sort through them all but one thing remains very clear to me. Ryan is the one thing that links these two deaths together. I'm not sure of his exact involvement or just how deep this goes but one thing I am certain of is that I am going to get to the bottom of this one way or another.

I pry one eye open and then the other, the buzzing next to my head stopping and then restarting again within seconds, officially pulling me from sleep. Swiping my hand next to me, I finally locate my phone, flipping it open without even looking at the caller I.D.

"Hello." I croak out, my voice thick with sleep.

"You realize it's two in the afternoon." Ryan's voice comes across the other line.

"Late night." I mutter, the events of the previous night hitting me like a bolt of lightning causing me to shoot up in my bed.

Looking around, I realize that I must have dozed off this morning without even realizing it. My laptop is still lying open next to me and I am still wearing the same dress I wore to Ryan's last night.

"Tell me about it." He chuckles, calming my sudden thumping heartbeat a small fraction. "I don't even remember falling asleep."

"That's probably the bottle of scotch we drank." I try to keep my voice as casual as possible.

"I guess so." He laughs lightly. "I feel like an ass for passing out on you, how about I offer a re-do. This time I promise I will lay off the scotch."

"I don't know. I have so much to do today." I hesitate, knowing if I don't accept it may raise some red flags but accepting could put me in a situation I am not prepared to be in yet.

"Oh come on. Don't leave a guy hanging." He playfully pleads.

"Well, I have been dying to try that new Italian

restaurant in the city." I suggest going out instead, offering me an easier means of escape.

"Rosiattos?" He asks, of course immediately knowing the name.

"Yeah I think that's it." I say, just wanting to meet somewhere public to appease him without having to commit to anything further.

"I'll pick you up at seven. Oh and Allie." He adds on. "Wear something sexy for me." He purrs, disconnecting the call before I have a chance to reply.

Tossing the phone down, I flop back down in my bed, letting out a long exhale as I let the events of the past few days really start to sink in.

My time with Luke.

My night with Ryan.

The flash drive that I am still not certain will amount to anything.

My date with Ryan tonight.

The wheels continue to turn as I try to hash all this out in my head. What if Ryan had something to do with Sarah's death? What if he is somehow responsible and found a way to cover it up? It wouldn't be the first time. But what if he had nothing to do with it at all? I can't help but feel like I am just spinning my wheels.

When I came here I had a clear cut path. Get close to Ryan, infiltrate his life, leak anything I could find that would expose him for the lying coward that he is. Only the deeper I look, the more I am starting to believe that I am just grasping to find something that isn't there.

And what about Nicholas Scott?

Is he really as bad as I initially believed or is he simply a father guilty of protecting his child? I was so positive coming in I knew the answer but now I'm not so sure.

The lines are blurred. There are so many different pieces to a puzzle that still doesn't quite fit together. I thought I understood what I was doing; now I feel like I'm not sure of anything.

And then there's Luke; a man that in one touch brought me back to life. In one kiss he showed me what life can be. When I close my eyes I can still feel his hands, the way my skin prickled when they traced my body.

The girl who used to feel nothing suddenly feels so much. I still can't believe how strong my feelings for him have become in such a short time. I feel like the moment I walked into his office everything started changing. He stirred something inside of me from that very first day, something that I was able to ignore until New York.

Am I really prepared to let him go forever?

Again, a question I thought I knew the answer to that I am now unsure of. Feeling lost is something I have grown accustomed to over the years but this is different somehow.

Before when I felt lost, I used my anger to anchor me. But for the first time in as long as I can remember I actually crave something beyond my revenge. I am fueled by something beyond my hatred. And deep down, I just don't know if I have it in me to keep going.

Chapter Twenty-four

Samantha

When Ryan pulls up outside of the Regency, I quickly exit the lobby, thankful that this time around I am not approached by any of the employees. Stepping out onto the sidewalk, I quickly slide into Ryan's car, hitting him with a smile the moment his face comes into view.

"Hey." I breathe, latching my seatbelt the moment I am situated.

"Hey." His reply is stiff.

I straighten my posture and look out of the passenger window, realizing almost immediately that something is off. Ryan is silent as he weaves in and out of traffic, his eyes never once leaving the road.

"So have you been to this restaurant before?" I turn towards him, just trying to ease the tension that seems to be swimming through the car.

"Do you think I'm stupid?" His question catches me off guard but he makes no attempt to look at me.

"I'm sorry?" I question, a wave of panic running through my spine.

"Me? Stupid? Is that what you think I am?" His voice is condescending and cruel and I immediately realize that he must know something, I'm just not sure what or how much.

"Not at all." I shake my head, trying to keep my façade firmly in place.

"Hmmm." The sound rolls off his tongue but he doesn't give me any other response.

"What's this about?" I question, not trying to hide my confusion.

"Why don't you tell me?" He flicks his eyes on me for the briefest moment.

That one look is enough to paralyze me right on the spot; sending fear flooding through me.

"I don't know." I choke out my response, for the first time since this conversation began actually taking the time to look out the window.

"Where are we going?" I ask, realizing that we are on the outskirts of the city.

"You'll see." A wicked smile turns up the corners of his mouth.

"Ryan, what is going on?" I don't try to hide the panic in my voice.

For the first time since starting this whole charade, I am actually scared for my well-being and I never considered that would be a position I would find myself in.

"Well since you seem to be so curious about me, I thought I would take you somewhere we can talk more privately. You know, where we can really get to know each other."

"I don't understand." I continue to try to fight through the fear, reassuring myself that this is all just a misunderstanding even though I am fairly certain it is not.

"Well since you feel like you need to steal from me

to find out about me, I thought I would give it to you first hand."

"Ryan… I" I immediately try to make an excuse but he cuts me off.

"Enough." His voice echoes through the car, rendering me silent. "It's my turn to talk now." He turns off into a warehouse parking lot, the area concealed by several run down brick buildings that seem to sit in an almost circle pattern.

Powering off the car, he turns slightly inward to face me.

"I have to say, I'm impressed. I have never had a girl actually drug me before." He laughs, shaking his head when I instinctively reach for the door handle, finding it locked.

"The great thing about being rich, you can customize anything." He laughs again when I pull at the handle, knowing by his statement that my attempts are futile.

"By all means keep trying. I kind of like watching you squirm." He cocks his head to the side, a sick smile turning up his mouth.

"How did you know?" I finally face the music, hoping there is still a chance I can get out of this situation unscathed.

"You think a man as rich and powerful as I am doesn't take certain precautionary measures?" He shakes his head slowly. "My entire apartment is wired with security cameras. Every. Single. Room." His smile widens.

"When I woke up this morning, at first I thought exactly what you wanted me to think; that we drank too much, we fucked and then we passed out. But the more I thought about it, the more I realized that I remembered nothing beyond drinking the glass of scotch that you poured for me. I decided to review the footage. Do you want to know what I found?" He pauses.

"I found you rummaging through my apartment after you had slipped something into my drink and then stripped me naked on my couch. I hope you enjoyed that, you're welcome." He winks causing my stomach to twist violently.

"I can explain." I start, but once again he doesn't let me finish.

"Not your turn yet." He ticks his finger at me. "When I realized you stole my flash drive, something clicked. I had my head of security do a little more digging and they came across the most interesting thing." He pauses for dramatic effect.

"What?" My voice is weak and broken, my hands shaking so violently that I can't even attempt to control it.

"They found out that Allie Reynolds, the one you claim to be, died two years ago. So unless you're just visiting from the grave, I think it's safe to say you're not Allie Reynolds. Isn't that right?" He pauses for a long moment.

"Samantha." He tacks on.

The back of his hand instantly connects with my mouth, knocking me backwards before I can react.

I don't have a chance to recover from the blow before his hand shoots out to grab the back of my head, tangling a handful of my hair in his fingers.

"You're as stupid as your fucking brother." He yells in my face before slamming my forehead into the dashboard of his car, the impact causing my head to ring violently.

"You should have left well enough alone Samantha. Now you've left me with no choice." He tisks his tongue, tightening the grip he has on my hair.

"Please let me go." I plead, tears clouding my vision as the pain in my head starts to spread. "Please."

"You really do think I'm stupid." He lets out a high pitched laugh.

I push at his chest, trying to free myself from his grip but he only tightens it more, the pull on my hair so intense I swear chunks must be ripping away from my scalp.

"Hold still honey, this will only hurt worse if you struggle." He says, my eyes catching sight of the syringe just moments before it plunges into the side of my neck, sending a pain shooting through me.

"I thought perhaps I should repay the favor." He says, pulling the needle from my flesh and holding the now empty syringe in front of me.

"What did you do?" I immediately feel the drowsiness start to set in.

"Why nothing you haven't done to me sweetheart." He says, patronizing me with his tone.

"What is happening?" I slur.

The inside of the car starts to spin slightly and my stomach lurches violently, panic taking a forefront just before I feel my body go limp and my mind start to fog.

"Nighty night Samantha." I hear Ryan's voice once more before everything fades to black.

Chapter Twenty-five

Samantha

I can taste iron. My mouth is cracked and dry. When I run my tongue along my lower lip I cringe at the sting the contact creates. Slowly opening my eyes, it takes only moments before I realize my hands are bound behind me, restrained by rope that appears to be twisted around both of my wrists.

My mind is a blur, trying desperately to piece together what happened and how I ended up here. Like flashes from a dream things slowly start coming into view; Ryan, the syringe he jammed into my neck, the fact that he now knows exactly who I am.

One thought and one thought only takes the forefront in my mind...

I have to get out of here.

I tug, realizing instantly that the rope is far too tight for me to try to slip my hands out. Lifting my head, for the first time since coming to, I finally look at my surroundings. I am in a dimly lit room that is bare of any furnishings. Something about this place seems oddly familiar and yet I can't seem to place it. That is, until I feel the sway of the floor below me.

I must be on the yacht, below deck somewhere. By the way, the vessel seems to be rocking in place it doesn't appear as though we are moving. Praying that we are still docked, I try lifting the chair I am bound to in an attempt to move.

It takes only seconds for me to realize that there is also a rope weaving around my ankles holding me against the legs of the chair I am sitting in. Trying to rock myself forward in an attempt to loosen the rope and to try and find a weak point, I immediately stop moving when the restraints on my wrists become so unbearably tight I can feel the rope tearing into my flesh. Relaxing back into the chair, I try to look behind me to see what exactly the chair is anchored to but my attention is pulled forward when I realize someone is coming.

I jump, my breathing immediately accelerating when I hear a nearby door open and close, followed by footsteps, each one getting closer and closer until the sound is just feet from me. When the door opens, I am temporarily blinded by the light that pours inside making it difficult for me to see anything.

It's daylight?

I feel like it's been only minutes since the moment I climbed into Ryan's car.

What time is it?

How much time has actually passed?

By the feeling of my body I would say I have been here for several hours but I can't be sure.

Ryan's chilling laugh immediately fills the space as the door latches closed behind him, the light dying off instantly making it easier for me to make out his face.

"You're awake." His voice is light and carefree like

everything is completely natural.

"Where am I? What is going on?" My panic shows through as I start to realize just how serious this situation is.

"Where you are doesn't matter. Now why... That's a bit of a different story." His laughter is haunting, causing fear to cripple me.

"Why are you doing this?" My voice is broken and hoarse, the words barely able to escape my lips.

I swallow hard, realizing how dry and painful my throat feels.

"Why am *I* doing this?" Ryan laughs again, grabbing a chair similar to the one I am sitting in, or maybe it's the same I can't be sure, before taking a seat just feet in front of me.

"I didn't do anything my dear Samantha, you did. You sealed your fate when you decided to take me on. You see, you're not the first to come after me but you're definitely the first to get this far. I will commend you for that." He tilts his head like he's truly impressed.

"Let me go." I demand, not willing to show him the weakness I feel inside.

"Or what?" He questions. "Tell me what could possibly happen to me if I don't? Because from where I am sitting, you are in no place to make demands."

"You won't get away with this." I threaten.

"But I already have. You've been gone for nearly two days and not one person even cares. I can't imagine what that must feel like for you." He taunts me. "What's that like Samantha? What's it like existing in a world where you know not one living soul cares if you live or die?"

"Fuck you." I spit, his behavior making my anger

flare from deep inside of me.

"Fuck me?" He clicks his tongue against the roof of his mouth.

Reaching out, he slides his fingertips across my chest, the feeling of his touch through the thin material of my dress causing a violent shutter to run through my body.

"Such a waste." He shakes his head slowly, dropping his hand away on a long pause.

I sit in silence, holding my breath, anticipating his next move.

"It's too easy really." He finally continues. "No one will even know you're gone. You did all the work for me. I mean, Allie Reynolds is already dead." His words send a panic that constricts my chest making it difficult to breath.

"It won't be like Sarah." He continues, smiling when he sees the shock and fear that display so clearly across my face.

"Still haven't put it together have you? And here I thought you had it all figured out." His wicked smile spreads.

"What did you do?" The words fall weakly from my lips.

"There you go putting it on me again." He shakes his head slowly back and forth, relaxing back into his chair as he crosses his arms in front of himself, his eyes remaining firmly fixed on my face.

"I don't understand why you just automatically assume that I am the bad guy here." He plays innocent, the smile on his face showing me he knows the truth.

"Because you are." My statement comes out thick, the words hard to form through the rawness of my throat.

"I guess from where you're sitting." He laughs lightly, clearly amused at seeing me in my current predicament. "Anyways, I digress." He continues.

"Sarah Trammell was a lot like you; young, beautiful, stubborn as hell. Well, at least until I stuck a needle in her arm. I'll never forget that feeling. Knowing that in that moment I had all the power. I could choose to save her or I could let her die and never have to worry about her causing problems for me again. I'm certain you can figure out what route I chose." His smile sickens me and it takes everything I have to keep my eyes on his face, fearful of what he will do if I don't give him the attention he so clearly expects right now.

"She deserved it." He continues without even a hint of remorse. "Telling her roommate I raped her and that she was going to go to the authorities. Hell, if I had let her live she would have seen to it that she destroyed me and any future I hoped to have. She had to go. She left me with no choice. Just another college student who couldn't take the pressure and turned to drugs to cope. No one even questioned it. Well, with the exception of your brother that is." He says, raising his eyebrows at me in a way that I can only describe as excitement.

"You see." He continues. "Sean knew her very well, so you can imagine his reaction when the girl he was head over heels for, who never did drugs, suddenly turned up dead of an overdose."

"He tried to piece it together of course. But with no proof, there was very little he could do. But that didn't stop him from poking around where he shouldn't have. What is it with you Cole siblings not being able to leave well enough alone?" He cocks his head to the side, his eyes burning holes into my face.

When I don't respond immediately, he continues

speaking like he didn't stop to ask the question at all.

"Sean started pushing the authorities to look further into Sarah's death and he wasn't quiet about it. Knowing I had to act fast, I invited Sean out for drinks, which was nothing out of the ordinary for us so obviously he thought nothing of my invite. After knocking a few back, Sean opened up to me about Sarah, even going as far as to tell me that he had proof her death was not an accidental overdose as it had been ruled. He truly believed she had been murdered but still hadn't pieced together who had done it. After that I knew what needed to be done. There was only one way I was going to be able to silence Sean Cole. So, being the good friend I was, I proceeded to pump him full of shots and then when he could barely hold his head up, I offered him a ride home, which he accepted. It wasn't until we got a few miles outside of the city that things took a turn. In his drunken state, he asked me in complete seriousness if I had something to do with Sarah's death. I didn't say yes but there must have been something in my reaction that made him believe it was me because within moments he was accusing me of killing her. He turned violent, demanding that I pull the car over. I guess we both know what happened next." He stops, gauging how that comment sits with me.

"You see my dear Samantha, the accident that killed your brother was actually his own fault. It ended up working out better for me in the end. Even if he had not grabbed the wheel and pulled us off the road that night, he was still going to meet the same fate." He smirks as tears flow freely down my face.

"You're a lot like your brother. You have good instincts but have a bad habit of making enemies of the wrong people. You could have had a long happy life and now you are doomed to the same fate as your brother. It's sad really." He shakes his head, his smile showing clearly that he's not the least bit sad.

"You're sick." I spit, anger boiling in my throat as I fight against my restraints.

"I do what I have to do to protect myself." His smugness turns to anger as he pushes his chair backwards, the wood skidding across the floor.

He steps towards me and violently grabs my face, squeezing so hard I feel like my cheekbones are going to cave in.

"You came at me remember? You started this. You have no one but yourself to blame." He screams in my face before shoving it to the side, his hand finally releasing its hold on me.

When I turn back towards him he is still hovering above me, his face just inches from mine.

"You know it is a shame really." He pauses, running his tongue along his lower lip. "The things I could have done to this body." He rasps, roughly pressing his lips to mine.

A cry sounds from my throat as pain shoots through my swollen bottom lip.

"Perhaps it's not too late." He breathes against my mouth before pressing harder into the kiss.

Panic floods through me, my mind struggling to find a way out of this situation. I try to turn my head but his hand shoots out, holding it in place. His other hand goes to my thigh, squeezing so tightly I open my mouth on another cry of pain.

"That's it baby." He purrs against my mouth.

I struggle against his advances, trying to fight

against his touch but my efforts get me nowhere. I am powerless to stop him. Powerless to keep his hand from traveling upwards and sliding inside of my panties, powerless to stop his fingers from jamming inside of me one and then two, the vicious nature of his touch sending pain spiraling through my body. He adds a third finger, thrusting it into me as he groans in pleasure, his face still just inches from mine as he stands over me.

"Fuck." He grinds out, increasing the speed of his hand.

"I am going to fuck you so hard Samantha." He breathes. "I'm going to fuck you and then..." He stills his hand inside of me. "Then I am going to kill you and toss you into the ocean." He smiles, pressing his mouth roughly against mine once more.

Desperately needing to find a way to stop his advances, I struggle against his touch, trying to squeeze my thighs together. He laughs at my efforts, shoving his fingers into me more forcefully as punishment for trying to fight him.

Finally I do the only thing I can think to do. I open my mouth and bite down on his bottom lip as hard as I can. His fingers immediately stop their assault, pulling out of me as he hollers in pain. Jumping backwards, he raises his hand to his now bleeding lip.

"You fucking bitch." He seethes.

He lays a hard backhanded slap to my face, the impact immediately bringing the taste of blood back to my mouth. Another hit, this one to the side of my head, renders me near unconscious but the feeling quickly fades and I look back up just in time for another blow to land just below my left eye.

I cry out from the pain, tears and blood now flowing freely down my face. Ryan stands above me for several long moments. I hold my breath, keeping my eyes tightly shut as I wait for the next hit to come.

I don't look up until I hear Ryan's voice, the sound so chilling it instantly paralyzes me with fear.

"I can't let you bleed too much sweet Samantha, at least not yet." He smiles, sliding his shirt off.

Twisting the material, he drapes it around my face, forcing the fabric between my lips before tying it tightly around the back of my head. The thickness of the material against my already dry tongue makes it hard to keep myself from gagging.

Ryan gives me a satisfied grin straightening his posture to look over his handy work. He jumps slightly when his cell phone starts buzzing in his pocket. Reaching for it, his sick smile spreads wider.

"It's your boyfriend." He shows me the name flashing across the screen.

Luke.

I try to scream through the fabric but it's too thick and my voice barely breaks the surface. Tears flow harder when Luke's face flashes through my mind. The thought of how he will react when he finds out the truth is crippling. Then again, if I know Ryan, no one will ever find out the truth. I'm not sure which thought scares me more.

"Don't you go anywhere." Ryan teases. "I have big plans for you." He promises as he backs slowly out of the room, putting the phone to his ear as he does.

Chapter Twenty-six

Luke

Pressing the call button for the fifth time in the last two hours, I hold the phone to my ear. It rings over and over again and like all the times before is met by a recorded message telling me the person I am calling is unavailable.

Dropping the phone onto my desk, I let out a frustrated sigh. Where the hell is she? It's nearly two o'clock and not only has Allie not shown up for work but I have been unable to reach her.

This is your own fault, I tell myself.

How long did I think she was going to hang around here with the way I have been treating her? At this point I don't know if I am more upset with her over the Ryan situation or if I am more pissed at myself for just rolling over and letting my brother have her.

She was worth fighting for.

She _is_ worth fighting for.

Picking up the receiver of my desk phone, I call Hannah in Human Resources and ask her to pull Miss Reynolds file for me. She agrees and I quickly hang up, grabbing my suit jacket off the back of my chair before heading out of my office.

"There must be some mistake." I stare back at the older woman across from me. "Her employment records list this as her address."

"I'm so sorry, Sir, but I have no one by that name listed in our system." The front desk receptionist of the Regency repeats her previous statement. "I'm afraid there's no mistake. The apartment number you have for her is currently occupied by a young couple and their infant son. There is no Allie Reynolds registered to any apartment in this building."

I want to argue with her, insist that she check again but I know that the attempt would be futile. It's clear that Allie lied on her paperwork, I'm just not sure why.

Thanking the woman for her help, I quickly turn and exit the lobby. Pulling out my cell I immediately call Travis, the head of security at ScoTech.

"Travis, it's Luke." I say the moment his voice comes on the line. "I need you to run an extensive check on my new assistant, Allie Reynolds. Hannah will be able to provide you with all the information she has on her. I already know that she lied about her residence. I need to know what else she's falsified."

"You got is boss." He responds without hesitation.

"Call me the minute you know anything." I instruct, ending the call before he has a chance to say anymore.

****

"So you're telling me you found nothing?" I stare back at Travis blankly, unable to believe what I am hearing. "How is that possible?" I question. "We ran a background check did we not? How are we just now learning that there is no recent record of this girl?"

"The background check human resources performs for standard employment is a simple social security check. They make sure it comes back stating *no criminal history on file* and leave it at that. Upon further inspection it appears as though a fake social security number was used." He states.

"Well whose social security number was it?" I demand, frustrated that I even have to ask.

"It belongs to a young woman who died two years ago. Her name was Allie Reynolds and she shares the exact same birthdate as the employee in question. I checked and verified the information this morning myself." His words take a moment to really sink in.

My mind races with the information, unable to process the notion that the woman I have spent the last five weeks falling for doesn't actually exist.

"I did a little more digging and found this." He says, sliding a photograph across the desk to me.

"What is this?" I ask, staring down at the picture of a young brunette girl standing in front of the main campus sign at Stanford.

"That is Allie Reynolds." He states, pointing to the young girl in the photo. "She graduated from Stanford four months before she was killed in a car accident."

"There must be some reasonable explanation." I finally speak, trying desperately to make myself believe my own statement.

"Perhaps, but I doubt it." Travis doesn't try to candy coat it for me. Being an ex-Marine, he is about as honest and honorable as they come.

"Advanced Global?" I question, just now remembering that Human Resources verified her internship there. Clearly she couldn't have falsified that too.

"Never worked there. In fact, when I called to speak to Ms. Osborne she claims she never received a phone call from us in regard to employment verification. So whoever they talked to wasn't her."

It takes everything in me to hold my shit together. Finding out someone you thought you knew is someone else entirely is one thing, having fallen for that person is quite another. I can't seem to accept the truth, even if it's all laid out right in front of me.

"What about an address?" I ask. "Did you have any luck pinpointing where exactly Miss Reynolds actually lives."

"We did find an apartment on the far side of the city leased under her name. I haven't had a chance to check it out yet." He adds.

"No need. Just give me the address and I'll take care of it."

"With all due respect Mr. Scott, I really think you should let me and my team handle this one. You have no idea who this girl actually is or what you're going to be walking into." He warns.

"I may not know who she really is but I know her.

I'm not in any danger I can assure you of that. If she meant to harm me she would have done so already." I say, my mind immediately flashing to the two nights I spent holding her in my arms.

"Even still, I don't recommend you going over there alone."

"I appreciate your concern Travis but I can handle this." I say. "Text me the address and I would appreciate this staying between us for the time being. Are we clear?"

"Yes Sir." He nods, standing and exiting my office without another word.

The moment the door snaps closed I go slack in my chair. I can't seem to grasp the reality of the situation taking place around me. How does someone falsify who they are and then keep up the façade so seamlessly for weeks?

It just doesn't add up. In the moments I spent with Allie, I didn't feel like she was pretending. If anything I feel like she let me in during our time in New York and showed me a side of herself that she doesn't show easily.

I can't let myself believe this was all a lie. I won't.

But then flashes of our last conversation come flooding to the surface.

Ryan...

This isn't about me at all. It's about my brother. I knew something didn't add up with the two of them. This is why. This is why Allie walked away from me for my brother. This is why I could sense that her heart wasn't in it. Because whatever she's up to, and why she's even here, has everything to do with Ryan.

Immediately going for my phone, I click on Ryan's name and wait impatiently as it rings over and over again. After what feels like an eternity his voice finally comes across the line.

"To what do I owe this pleasure?" His sarcasm bleeds through his voice.

"I'm looking for Allie. She hasn't shown up at the office and I can't get ahold of her, I was hoping maybe you had talked to her." I state, not yet ready to share the information I have learned with my brother.

"Haven't seen her." He replies casually.

"So you haven't talked to her at all?" I question.

"She was at my place Friday but we didn't do much talking if you know what I mean." His words send a weight crashing down on my chest, the impact making it difficult to find my breath.

"But you haven't talked to her since?" I push on.

"No, but then again you know how I am. One and done." He laughs, stirring the anger that has been building silently inside of me throughout the course of the day. "So she didn't show. I'm sure you can find someone to fill her position in no time."

"That's not what I'm worried about." I grind out through my teeth.

"What? Hoping you could hop on for some sloppy seconds? I gotta say, you must be getting desperate Luke."

"Fuck you Ryan, stop playing games. Have you honestly not talked to her?" I bite, unable to tolerate my brother's ridiculous nonsense any further.

"Calm down Luke I'm just messing with you. No, I have not talked to her but I will let you know if I do."

"Make sure you do." I clip, ending the call instantly.

Ryan may not be able to tell me where Allie is but I know for one hundred percent certainty that he is somehow tied to her being here in the first place.

I just need to find out why…

Chapter Twenty-seven

Samantha

My eyes feel weighted, like they are being held closed. I struggle to open them. I struggle to keep them open once I manage to get them there. I can feel myself fading in and out of consciousness, unable to find the strength to fight any longer.

The flesh on my wrists is torn and tattered from trying to work the ropes loose. I can't see them but I can feel it. I can feel the jagged skin catch painfully every time I move; I can feel the blood running down my hands.

I need to fight, I know I do, but the moment I wrap my mind around the thought the blackness takes me under again.

Finally managing to get my eyes open, the room is barely visible. My vision is blurred making it difficult for me to focus on any one thing. My head bobs a little before I find the strength to finally hold it completely upright.

I can hear his footsteps above, one after another. They never stop. He never leaves. I tense when I hear him coming again. His steps echoing through the otherwise silent room, becoming louder the closer he gets.

Slumping my head back down, I pretend to be unconscious, hoping that he will simply leave but prepared to fight if he doesn't. I hear him enter, holding my breath with each painfully slow step he takes towards me until I feel him stop directly next to me.

"It won't be long now my dear." I hear him rasp in my ear, his breath hot on the side of my face. "But just to be sure you don't cause any problems." I hear him say just moments before the jab of the needle hits my neck.

The sudden pain makes me jump which prompts Ryan's laughter to fill the room just as everything once again fades to black.

I strain through the silence, trying to check for signs that Ryan is nearby before I attempt to pull my eyes open. I can hear nothing; nothing beyond the occasional creak of the floor below me and the faint sound of the water lapping around the sides of the boat.

For a moment I wonder if I am still alive, if I am still here. When Ryan stuck the needle in my neck this last time I thought for sure that would be it; that I would never wake up again. But I guess I should have known better. He's not done toying with me yet.

By this point he could have killed me, disposed of my body, and returned to his normal life like nothing had even happened. It's his spitefulness and his need to hurt me that will ultimately be his downfall. I'm not ready to die, but if I do I am going to make damn sure I take Ryan Scott down with me.

Lifting my head, my neck is nearly unable to support the weight and I struggle once again to keep it upright. I have no concept of time. No real idea of how long I have been down here, beaten and deprived of food and water.

I know that if I want any hope of making it out of here alive that I have to find a way out of the restraints. I cry out when I twist my wrist, the shirt wedged between my lips muffling the sound as I pull harder and harder against the rope binding me to the chair.

Tears flood my vision as I continue pulling and twisting against the rope, each movement becoming more painful than the last until I am convinced that I can take no more. Refusing to give up, I fight through the pain. I fight past the tears and through the rip of my skin as it tears against the ropes.

Minutes pass, one after another, each as painful as the last but I am determined to not just sit here and let Ryan kill me. I won't let him win... Not this time.

I cry out both in pain and relief when I finally

manage to get my left hand free. A rush of adrenaline suddenly kicks in and I am twisting and yanking at the ropes, finally managing to also free my right hand. Still in disbelief that my hands are actually free, I immediately remove my gag and make for the ropes around my ankles.

I find it much easier to free my legs since I can use my fingers to untie the knots. Even still, it takes me several minutes to finally remove the last of my restraints. When I manage to pull myself into a stand, my entire body revolts the movement and I collapse down onto the floor, so weak I can barely find the strength to stand.

Taking a deep breath, I manage to find strength from somewhere deep inside of me and push myself back up. Whether it is my family or simply my will to live, I don't know, but something is driving me, willing me to escape.

I breathe a sigh of relief when I realize the door to the room is not locked. Clearly Ryan didn't think there was any chance of me breaking free from the restraints, especially considering he's kept me drugged nearly this entire time.

Pushing my way out of the room, I stumble up the shallow staircase to the surface above, collapsing onto the deck the moment I reach it.

Even in the darkness of the night I can see that Ryan is not on board. My heart begins pumping faster than I think it ever has before the moment I realize that we are still docked at the marina, that there is still a chance that I can make it out of here.

Taking a deep breath, I crawl on my hands and knees towards the dock, more determined than ever before to make it off this boat and out of the clutches of Ryan Scott.

Stumbling down the ramp, I hit the dock on a loud

thud, my legs not able to support my own weight from the steep step down. Pushing back up, I run as fast as my body will allow down the dock, my bare feet sounding lightly against the wood with each step I take.

I finally reach the gate that separates the private dock from the marina but before I can make a move I am paralyzed by the sound of oncoming footsteps. I know it's Ryan. I can feel it in the fear that slowly creeps up my back the closer the footsteps get to me.

Before the approaching individual comes into view, I quickly drop to the ground and roll behind a boat trailer parked just feet from the gate, holding my breath as I listen to the footsteps get closer. My heart is thumping inside of my chest so loudly I swear there's no way that he won't be able to hear it. It beats viscously against my ribcage as I wait through each painfully slow second that ticks by.

It isn't until the person passes the trailer that I turn my head to the side and chance a look in their direction, a violent shudder running through me the moment my fear is confirmed.

It is Ryan.

He's got a bag in one hand and his other tucked into his jacket. I barely get a good glimpse at him before he begins fading into the darkness, the dim overhead lamps offering very little light. Knowing it will be only moments before he steps on board and realizes I am gone, I have to act now.

Pushing up, I keep my body hunched over as I slip through the gate and out into the main part of the marina. I run as quickly as I can, which in my current state equates to a slow jog, my legs having trouble supporting my own weight given the weakness of my body.

My face is swollen and my throat is so dry that I find it impossible to do something as simple as swallow. My gray sleeveless shift dress is ripped at the bust and torn slightly at the bottom, the front covered in blood though I can't be sure where exactly it came from.

Ryan is sure to have realized I am gone by now and I know I have not made it as far as I need to. For someone who may be looking for me I stand out like a sore thumb. I am lucky enough to have the night on my side but at the same time, the darkness and absence of people makes me even more anxious.

I stop at every vehicle that is parked on my way out, checking each one to see if it is locked or if anyone left their keys inside. I know it's a long shot but it's the only one I've got right now.

Every noise makes me jump as I weave through the marina. Every corner I turn I swear I see Ryan behind me. I need to find a way back to the city.

I don't know if I can risk going back to my apartment on the off chance that Ryan has figured out my actual residence but I truly have nowhere else I can go. Everything I have is there, including what little money I have saved.

Slipping in between two vehicles needing to rest, I hunch over trying to catch my breath and figure out my next move. I have nothing. No money, no phone, no way of reaching my apartment. I have no idea what I am going to do next.

Looking into the truck directly in front of me, my heart picks up speed when I realize that the keys are inside. For a moment I consider climbing into the truck and just disappearing. Simply slipping off into the night and never looking back. Leaving would be easier. But leaving this all behind also means I would be leaving Luke. Knowing what I now know about Ryan, there is no way I can do that.

Ryan is a murderer. Now more than ever I have to see this through. If I don't, all of this will have been for nothing and I can't accept that.

Sliding into the driver's seat of the run down pickup truck, I close the door as quietly as possible, immediately reaching for the keys. The moment the truck grumbles to life I throw it into gear, knowing that if Ryan spots me, he can easily trail me wherever I go.

I know stealing a car is probably not the best choice but right now I am in survival mode. I just need to get out of here. I make it out of the marina within seconds, the wheels of the truck screeching as I pull out onto the street too quickly. I am so lightheaded and disoriented that I find my perception is a bit off.

I pass a convenience store on my way out of town. For a brief moment I consider stopping to call the police but then immediately dismiss the idea. They would probably have him in custody in the matter of minutes but that doesn't mean that's where he would stay.

I may know the truth about Sarah and Sean but that doesn't mean I have any proof. I am also sure that Ryan will have erased any trace that I was ever on the boat by the time the police could get there. I know I don't have a leg to stand on. And if Ryan Scott has taught me anything it's that there's nothing he can't either talk or buy his way out of.

If I want to end this, I have to end it my way.

I can't help but look behind me every few seconds to make sure that I am not being followed. I tense with every pair of headlights I see and sometimes even convince myself that it's Ryan. I try to shake off the fear that continues to control my mind and keep my focus on what's to come.

My body is exhausted and I know I have demanded too much out of it tonight. And unfortunately I am going to have to ask for more.

Ryan is not going to just let me go so easily. If he knows where I live, I'll be lucky if he's not already there. If he doesn't, it won't be long before he figures it out. My window of time is very small. I need to get home, pack a few things, grab some cash, and disappear for a little while until I can sort all of this out and figure out my next move.

I just hope it's not already too late.

Chapter Twenty-eight

Luke

Westwood Apartment Complex is a rundown building that sits just on the edge of downtown. In the late evening darkness it looks more like an old warehouse than a building people actually live in. It houses about thirty apartments, most of which are occupied by less than desirable inhabitants. This is a rough part of town and just the thought of Allie living here makes me nervous.

The hallway paint is chipped and peeling. The carpet is stained and worn. In the two minutes it takes me to reach Allie's door I overhear two different shouting matches and one apartment that sounds as though five babies are inside screaming profusely.

Raising my fist to the tattered wood door with the crooked number sixteen screwed into it, I knock lightly, listening closely for any signs of someone inside. Several moments pass before I raise my hand and knock again, this time much louder.

Nothing…

Reaching out, I twist the knob, surprised to find it unlocked. Why would anyone leave their apartment unlocked in this type of neighborhood? Finding it odd, fear instantly creeps into the pit of my stomach as I push the door open, not yet sure of what to expect.

I let out a slow exhale as I step inside, closing the door behind me. The apartment is quiet and appears to be empty. Flipping on a nearby light switch, the moment the room comes into view my stomach twists again.

It makes me ill to think that Allie has been living here for God knows how long. The apartment is tidy and seems well kept but that doesn't make up for the peeling paint, stained floors, or the fact that the entire apartment is one square room.

There's a small kitchen, if that's what you would call it, along the same wall as the door. Two mattresses stacked on top of each other in the far left corner, and a ratty old couch sitting along the back wall. There is nothing here that ties Allie to the space. No pictures, no décor, just four blank walls.

In fact, the only thing in the entire room outside of the very few pieces of furniture is a half painted canvas propped on a stand in front of the only window in the apartment. Crossing the space, the moment I get close enough to really study the painting I am immediately in awe. The talent of the artist is so blindingly clear.

I had no idea Allie painted and the thought saddens me more than I expect it to. There is so much about this girl I don't know, so much I want to know.

Reaching out, I trail my fingers lightly across the paint strokes. I can envision Allie standing here, an old ratty paint stained t-shirt covering her petite frame, her hair pulled away from her face, her forehead scrunched together as she concentrates on the canvas in front of her.

The thought even manages to bring a smile to my face. That is until I remember that the girl I am envisioning doesn't actually even exist. A stranger lives here. A stranger painted this incredible piece. A stranger...

A loud thud behind me immediately pulls my attention to the door and I spin just in time to catch sight of a bloody Allie as she stumbles inside. She barely makes it two steps before she catches sight of me, stopping mid-step as she stares back at me, her entire face frozen with fear.

"Allie?" I barely get out, my voice getting lost somewhere in the air.

I only get a glimpse of her swollen face before she turns away from my gaze.

Showing next to no reaction to finding me standing in her apartment, she stumbles through the space like she is heavily intoxicated. It's clear to see she's injured, I just don't know the extent and I didn't get a good enough look at her face to really assess the situation.

Crossing to the kitchen, she retrieves a glass from the cabinet before turning on the water, her hands shaking so badly that she drops it before she can even get it filled. It pings around the sink before shattering, the sound ringing through the small room.

Reaching for another glass, she manages to get this one filled before lifting it to her lips and draining the contents in the matter of seconds. I stand frozen, not sure how to react, as she fills the glass again and drains it as well, drinking like she hasn't done so in days.

"We have to get out of here." She finally speaks, letting the glass roll out of her hand into the sink.

She stumbles across the room without even a glance

in my direction, stopping in front of a small door that sits along the left wall next to the two mattresses that are stacked on top of each other.

"Allie." I repeat, taking a step towards her as she slides open the door and pulls out a duffel bag from the small closet, tossing it onto the bed.

"He's coming." Her voice trembles as she pulls things from the closet and shoves the items haphazardly inside the bag, not once facing me.

"Who's coming?" I ask, trying to keep my distance.

It's clear something is very wrong here.

"I have to go. I have to leave. He's coming. He's coming." She chants, clearly disoriented.

Zipping the bag, she tosses it over her shoulder before making a break for the door. Catching up to her just as she pulls the handle, I place my palm against the wood blocking her escape.

"Let me go." She cries, pulling viciously at the handle. "Please." Her word is a sob that breaks off in her throat. "I don't have much time."

From my view point I can see that her dress is ripped and stained with blood. The side of her face has a bloody gash down it and she has several small bruises peppering her neck. It isn't until I see the bloody mess around her wrists that I realize something is really wrong.

"Hey." I say softly, trying to soothe her.

The moment my hand rests on her shoulder she jumps, clearly terrified.

"I won't hurt you." I reassure her, once again resting my hand on her shoulder in an effort to somehow comfort her.

"Allie what is going on? Who did this to you?" I ask, trying to make her face me.

Sobs rake through her body and she collapses

forward into the door, too weak to continue to fight.

"I have to get out here." She beats weakly against the wood. Her words are so blurred by the emotion in her voice that I am barely able to understand her.

"Please, you have to get me out of here." She turns towards me, offering me my first real look at her face.

I take a ragged inhale at the sight, all the air leaving my body in an instant.

Her entire face is swollen, blood stained and bruised. The gash on the side of her face is just the start. Her bottom lip is split and about three times its normal size. Her left eye is near black, another large gash just below it. She has a bloody knot on the right side of her forehead and other small bruises peppered across her jaw and cheekbones.

The sight of her literally makes it difficult to breathe. Anger and rage seethe through me and I am momentarily blinded by the heaviness of those emotions.

"Allie who did this to you?" I demand, placing my hands on both of her shoulders.

She mumbles, her eyes unable to hold my focus as she sways from side to side. Her lips are moving but I can't make out what she's saying. Suddenly she slumps forward and I have to scramble to prevent her from falling to the floor.

Wrapping my arms around her, I pull her into my chest, securing her against me. She trembles in my arms causing fear to cripple me. I need to get her to a doctor.

"I have to get out of here." Her words are barely audible against my chest.

"I'm taking you to the hospital." I say, sliding her

bag off of her shoulder and onto mine.

"No, you can't. He will find me there." She mumbles, her consciousness slipping.

"Who will find you Allie? Who did this?" I ask again, desperate to know the answer.

She whispers something but I can't make out her words. Lowering my head down, I ask her again.

"Allie who did this to you?"

Her whispered word is one the instantly paralyzes me.

"Ryan." She barely gets the name out before she goes slack in my arms.

Chapter Twenty-nine

Luke

Carrying Allie inside of my Santa Monica beach house, I turn to lock the door and arm the alarm the moment I step into the foyer. I am still not convinced that Ryan is the one responsible for this but I am not willing to take any chances where her safety is concerned. I need to make sure he can't just walk in without me at least being alerted the moment he does.

She stirs slightly in my arms as I cross the space, her eyes flickering open and closed as I carry her up the stairs to the bathroom. Pushing my way inside the large space, I gently set her on top of the counter before guiding her into a sitting position.

Even with her eyes open she doesn't seem alert and appears to be unable to support her own body as she sways slightly when I release her. Setting her duffel bag next to her, I tilt her head up so that she is forced to look at me.

"I know you're tired." I speak softly, trying to be as soothing as possible. "But I need to look at you." I say, getting a glossy eyed nod from her in return.

Grabbing the hem of her tattered dress, I work it up over her hips before sliding it over her head. She groans softly in pain but does her best to hold herself upright. Sitting in front of me in nothing more than a pair of black panties, I breathe a sigh of relief when I realize that the majority of her injuries I've already seen.

She has dark bruises up and down both of her arms but otherwise seems in pretty good shape considering. She has dark markings around her ankles and her wrists are lined with severe rope burn, her flesh torn away, a clear sign that whoever did this to her had her tied up.

"Can you sit here by yourself?" I ask, tipping her face back up when her head droops down slightly.

She nods, dryly licking her cracked swollen lip.

"I'm going to run you a bath and then I will get you something to drink." I say, turning away from her to cross the room to the bathtub.

Turning on the faucet, I find a comfortable temperature before adding a lavender bubble cream.

When I turn back towards her, she seems so disoriented and weak; the sight of her fragile bruised body makes it difficult for me to keep my anger contained. And while I desperately want to get to the bottom of this, I know right now I need to give her time.

At this point I have only two things to go on; one, Allie Reynolds is not the girl sitting in front of me and two, according to her my brother is the one who did this to her, I just haven't figured out why. It's hard to piece together a puzzle when you have so many missing pieces.

Crossing back towards the counter, I lift Allie up and set her gently to her feet. When my hands drop to the waistband of her panties she immediately jumps.

"I'm just helping you get into the tub. I won't even

look, I promise." I say, giving her a reassuring smile.

I hold eye contact with her as she steps out of her panties one leg at a time, her hands gripping my biceps for support. Once she is completely naked I guide her towards the large garden tub, offering her my hand for balance as she steps in, her legs clearly very weak.

She cringes when the warm water and suds engulf her body, the contact clearly painful on her still fresh wounds.

"I am going to give you some privacy." I say, slowly starting to back out of the room.

"Luke." Her weak voice finally breaks the surface. "Will you stay with me?" She turns her head to the side, her glossy tear filled eyes enough to gut me right here on the fucking spot.

"I'm not going anywhere, I promise. Let me just run downstairs and get you water and a little something to eat." I say, waiting until she gives me a weak nod before exiting the room.

In the time it takes me to make Allie a sandwich and cut her a couple pieces of fresh fruit, she is already out of the tub when I get back upstairs. Tied in the bath towel I set out for her, she is curled up in the fetal position in the middle of my bed clutching a pillow.

"Allie?" I approach slowly, not wanting to startle her.

I get no response and when I finally reach the bed it's clear to see why. She is passed out cold, her breathing even, her wet hair spread out on the bed behind her. I can't help the warm feeling that floods through me at the sight of her here, in my home, in my bed.

Setting the food and bottle of water down on the nightstand, I quietly back out of the room, flipping off the light before pulling the door closed behind me.

"You're up." I look up from my laptop just in time to see Allie enter the room, now dressed in a white tank top and black yoga pants.

Glancing to the clock, I see that it is just after three in the morning. I hadn't realized it was so late.

"Thank you for the food." She says, nervously tugging at the hem of her tank top as she stands in the doorway.

"I was worried it wouldn't be any good." I say, considering it's been sitting up there for over a couple of hours.

"It was perfect. Thank you."

"Do you feel any better?" I ask, closing my laptop before sliding it onto the coffee table in front of me.

"I do, thank you." She says, crossing the space towards me.

Opting to sit in the oversized chair across from me rather than joining me on the couch, she pulls her knees up to her chest and hugs them tightly against herself.

"What were you doing at my apartment?" She speaks again before I have a chance to, for the first time since entering the room looking at me head on.

She is still swollen and bruised but looks a hundred times better than she did a few hours ago.

"When you didn't show up for work Monday I went to the Regency to look for you. Needless to say I found out you didn't actually live there. I had my security team track down your actual address."

"I'm sorry." She immediately apologizes. "I never meant to involve you in any of this."

"In any of what Allie, or is that even your name?" I ask, leaning forward to rest my elbows on my knees.

"No." She sighs, breaking eye contact to look down.

"I think I deserve the truth." I say, my comment bringing her gaze back up to mine. "Don't you?"

"You won't understand." She says, tears immediately pooling in her eyes.

"Try me." I challenge. "Tell me who you really are."

"My name…" She fidgets nervously, crossing and uncrossing her feet as she sits curled in the chair.

"My name." She takes a deep breath. "Is Samantha Cole."

"Samantha Cole…" I let the name linger on my lips, knowing I have heard it somewhere before.

Before I can comment, she continues.

"My older brother was Sean Cole." She says, the familiarity of her name now ringing loudly through my ears.

That's where I've heard it before.

"Wait, so your brother…" I start, but she cuts me off.

"Was the one who died in the car accident caused by

Ryan." She confirms, her voice weak and shaky. "Allie Reynolds was a twenty-two year old graduate of Stanford that died a couple of years ago. When I moved to L.A. I needed a new identity so I chose one that I knew would allow me to secure employment with ScoTech. She had the right qualifications and was close enough to the same age that no one would question it. Her family all lives in Wyoming so I knew I could get away with it." She takes a long pause.

"As I said, my name is Samantha; my family always called me Sam. I grew up outside of Boise, Idaho. I am nineteen years old. I have never attended college. I have never worked anywhere outside of ScoTech. I basically lied about every aspect of who I am." She stops, hitting me with a worried expression.

"So none of it was true?" I ask, struggling through the fog that seems to be forming around me.

"It was with you." She says weakly. "I may have lied about my name, where I live, my education, but I never lied to you about who I really am. You saw me, really saw me. For the first time in my entire life I didn't feel like I needed to hide *me*. I know this makes no sense but I need you to understand *that* above anything. You gave me peace Luke, even if it was for just a short piece of time, and for that I will be eternally grateful." She swipes at a stray tear that manages to escape her eye.

I stay rooted to the spot, forcing myself not to run to her aid. I feel betrayed and honestly, really fucking daft, but at the same time I can't deny how deeply my feelings run for this girl, no matter what she's lied about.

"I don't understand though. Why did you come here in the first place? Why lie about who you are? What's your end game?" I ask, knowing she is only giving me a very small portion of the whole story.

"To understand the present, you have to first know the past. The night Sean died, my entire world fell apart. My parents didn't know how to cope, nothing made sense anymore. Two years passed in a fog of grief. When I was thirteen I found my mother dead of a drug overdose." She pauses, trying to calm the flow of tears now streaming down her face.

When I make a move to stand she holds her hand up, gesturing for me not to. The pain suddenly surging through me is enough to bring me to my knees. Having lost a mother, having watched her take her last breath as I held her hand, I know there is no greater pain.

"She hadn't been the same since Sean died." She fights through her emotion. "When I found her, I remember holding her against me, screaming at God to give her back, but she was gone. And while I was blinded by shock and pain, a small part of me felt relief; relief that she was at peace, relief that she would no longer have to mourn the loss of her son, relief that I would no longer have to see her in pain."

"I'm so sorry." The words barely make it past my lips.

"Things only got worse after Mom. My dad didn't know how to function without her. He tried for my sake but I knew he was giving up a little more every day. He stopped taking care of himself, he just stopped caring. He died less than four years later of a heart attack. I was seventeen." She wipes her cheeks with the back of her hand, trying to clear the fallen tears.

"At seventeen, you can't imagine the amount of pain and rage that had brewed inside of me over the years.

Every time I would close my eyes I would see my mother's limp lifeless body, I would see my father lying on the hospital table, his lips tinted blue. And you know who I blamed for all of it?" She asks, finally meeting my gaze straight on.

"Ryan." I say his name aloud.

"Ryan." She confirms. "It ate at me that my entire family crumbled and he walked away from the entire incident with a slap on the wrist. For years I watched his happy carefree life take flight while I was forced to endure the deepest depths of hell every day. After I lost my dad, something snapped. I knew the only way I would ever feel peace would be to make him pay the way he should have all those years ago." She pauses, letting out a slow controlled exhale.

"I never planned to physically hurt him; I could never hurt someone like that. But I knew a man like Ryan was bound to have some dirt lying around and I set out to find it. I wanted to ruin him. I wanted to drag his name through the mud and show the world what a spineless selfish man he is. I wanted to make him feel even an ounce of the pain he had caused me. That's why I applied for ScoTech. That's why I changed my identity. Because I knew I would never get anywhere close to him the moment he realized who I was."

"But then I learned the truth." She tries to control the quiver of her lip as she speaks. "That Ryan Scott is so much more than the spoiled rich playboy I had him pegged as."

"What do you mean?" I question when she abruptly stops.

"Ryan…" She stutters over the name. "Your brother." Another long pause. "He's a murderer." She says, the accusation causing me to suck in a sharp breath.

"What?" I question, my knee jerk reaction is to not believe her.

"Why do you think he did this to me?" Her voice goes up an octave as she pushes her legs to the floor and gestures to herself. "Why do you think he beat me and tied me up on his yacht?"

"How long?" I ask the question, not sure that I want to know the answer. When she hits me with a confused look I clarify. "How long did he have you there?"

"What day is today?" She asks.

"It's Tuesday." I answer.

"Tuesday." She seems surprised by my answer. "Saturday night." She shakes her head like she can't quite wrap her mind around it.

"He's had you on the yacht since Saturday?" I ask in disbelief.

Nodding, she continues. "He beat me, he molested me, and he planned to kill me." Her voice is almost hysterical at this point and it's clear by the fear etched so perfectly across her face that she is telling the truth.

"It's because I found out the truth. He killed Sarah Trammell." She says. "He raped her and then when she threatened to expose him he killed her and made it look like an accidental overdose. My brother started piecing it together and when he got too close to the truth, Ryan tried to kill him too. Only Sean realized it and tried to fight Ryan. That's what caused the car crash that killed my brother; he was fighting back." Her tears are back but this time they are more of anger than of pain.

"He couldn't…" I shake my head, pushing into a stand. "He wouldn't." I try to rationalize the situation.

"He did." She says so calmly that an immediate silence falls over the room.

"Then why have you not called the police? Why is he not behind bars right now?" I ask, none of this making much sense.

"Because I have no proof. I learned the truth because he told me. Of course, this was only after he had me in his grasp. He told me everything and I know he did so because he wanted me to die knowing that he won."

"But what he did to you, you have proof of that." I gesture to her face.

"But do I?" She questions. "He's cleared the yacht by now, there's likely no sign that I was ever there. At this point it would be my word against his. Sure maybe they would arrest him, throw him in jail for the night, but then what happens tomorrow when they are forced to release him because they don't have enough to hold him? No, I can't involve the police, not yet, not until I have the proof I need."

Several moments pass as I stand frozen staring back at Samantha, a girl I only just met and yet deep down feel like I truly know. She wouldn't lie about this.

"New York." I start, but she doesn't let me get any further.

"Were the best two days of my life." She says, slowly pushing into a stand, her tired body not able to move too abruptly.

"I never wanted Ryan, only to get close enough to find his weakness. Every moment I spent with him was torture, especially after New York. My mind knew I had to keep going, I had to see my plan through. But not a moment went by that I didn't think of you, that I didn't wish things were different. I never anticipated feeling this way about someone, especially the brother of the man I was trying to destroy." She walks slowly towards me.

"You have to believe me Luke. I never meant to pull you into all of this. It just happened and I couldn't stop it."

"Did you sleep with him?" The words leave my lips just as she stops a couple of feet in front of me.

"No." She answers, the response causing relief to flood through me. "I just needed him to believe I would."

"Where is Ryan now?" I ask, finally coming back to the current situation at hand.

"Probably out looking for me." She shudders at the thought.

"Don't worry." I say, immediately reaching for her and pulling her into my arms. "I promise you, I won't let him hurt you." I say, kissing the top of her head. "You're safe here. When I'm done with my brother, he won't be able to ever hurt you again."

"Don't go after Ryan." She says, stepping back to look up at me, her bruised face a gut wrenching reminder of what my brother did to her.

"I can't just let him get away with this." I can feel the anger bubbling in my throat.

"And he won't." She gives me a weak smile. "I just need some time. If he tries to contact you, he needs to think everything is completely normal. You can't lead on like anything is wrong, otherwise he will know something is up. Please." She reaches up, trailing her hand lightly down the side of my face.

"For you." I answer, not able to resist the urge to lean down and brush my lips lightly against hers, careful not to put too much pressure on her injured lip.

"Thank you." She breathes when I rest my forehead

gently against hers. "You know the thing I was the most afraid of through this whole ordeal was not failing or even dying for that matter; it was the thought of losing you that scared me the most."

"You're not going to lose me Samantha." I reassure her, seeing the way her eyes immediately glaze over.

"Say it again." She gives me a tear filled smile.

"You aren't going to lose me." I repeat, not able to fight my own smile.

"No, my name." She sniffs.

"Samantha." I say, pulling her back into my arms.

Chapter Thirty

Samantha

"You okay?" Luke slips in behind me, wrapping his arms around my waist, securing my back against his chest.

"Better." I hum when he places a feather light kiss to the side of my neck. "It's incredible here." I gesture out towards the ocean, the view from the outdoor balcony simply breathtaking.

Luke's house is unlike anything I have ever seen, or even imagined for that matter. It's an incredible two story beach house sitting just a few hundred feet from its own private beach. There's an oceanfront living and dining area with a wall of glass overlooking the water, and a chef style kitchen I swear my mother would have lived in. But it's the master suite that is the real treasure. I spent most of last night sitting on its private balcony that overlooks the ocean.

I even left the French doors that connect to the bedroom wide open when I curled into the bed next to Luke, finding the openness soothing after being restrained and shut away from the outside world for three days. There is something so peace invoking about falling asleep with the smell of the sea in your nose and the sound of the waves in your ears.

"This is my favorite spot." Luke finally speaks again, tightening his grip on me as he drops his chin to rest on my shoulder.

"I can see why." I grip the railing in front of me, breathing in the sea air. "And I can see why you couldn't bear to part with this house. It's like your own little piece of heaven up here."

"That's what my mom used to say." I can hear the smile in his voice which warms my heart.

I never imagined that this is where I would end up. I thought for sure the moment Luke found out the truth he would never want anything to do with me again. It means so much that not only has he been able to forgive the way I deceived him, he has also managed to give me a small glimmer of peace despite everything else going on.

I know Ryan is out there. I know he's not going to just let me go. But right now none of that matters. Nothing matters outside of this, outside of Luke and this moment and how he makes me feel.

The breeze whips around us causing a light shiver to run through me. Luke immediately runs his hands down my arms in an effort to warm me.

"It's getting pretty late." He observes, straightening his posture behind me. "We should probably head inside."

"Okay." I agree, turning away from my amazing view to look up at one that is equally amazing.

Luke catches my gaze and gives me a sweet smile, tucking away a stray strand of hair that blows in front of my face, his hand lingering for a long moment just below my ear.

"Thank you." He finally speaks, looking at me in a way that causes another shiver to run through me, this one for a completely different reason.

"For what?" I ask, confused by his statement.

"For trusting me." He says simply. "I know you must be terrified with everything that's going on. I can only imagine what it must take for you to put your faith in someone else with all you've been through. It just means a lot that you believe in me so much."

"I should be the one thanking you." I lay my hand lightly against his chest, loving the feeling of his beating heart beneath my palm. "I don't know where I would be if it wasn't for you." I answer truthfully.

"Come on." He says. "You look exhausted." He kisses the tip of my nose before taking my hand and leading me back inside the house.

I jump slightly when his cell starts ringing just moments after he slides the door closed behind us. He crosses the living area to where his phone is sitting on the coffee table, his nose curling slightly the moment he catches sight of the screen.

With that one look I know exactly who it is. I suddenly feel winded, like the floor has just dropped out from underneath me. I knew this would happen eventually. It was only a matter of time before Ryan reached out to his brother. I guess I was just hoping I could pretend that things were okay for just a little while longer.

Luke looks down at the screen for a long moment before hitting silence and dropping the phone back onto the table. When he looks back towards me he must see the panic etched across my face because he immediately rushes towards me, both of his hands coming to rest at the sides of my face the moment he reaches me.

"He will not hurt you." He reassures me, tilting my chin upwards to meet his gaze.

I muster a weak smile and a nod, trying to fight down the fear that slowly creeps into every pore of my body.

"Look at me Sam." Luke demands when my gaze falls away. "I won't let him." He whispers, his words playing lightly across my lips as he lowers his mouth to mine.

I know what he's doing. He's trying to distract me, give me something to focus on. And honestly, it works. The moment the contact is made, everything else falls away. My rapid heartbeat is no longer out of fear but out of desire. My skin no longer burns with panic but sizzles beneath the fire of Luke's touch.

Wrapping my arms around his neck, I pull him tighter, begging him to take it all away. The fear, the pain, take it all until there is nothing left but the way he makes me feel.

He deepens the kiss but his touch remains soft against my still swollen lip. His hands drop away from my face and before I can even react, are at the back of my thighs lifting me into his arms. Wrapping my legs around his waist, I tangle my fingers in his dark hair, tugging gently as I savor his taste, his smell, the feeling of his hard body against mine.

I feel each step he takes as he takes it, my body shifting slightly as he climbs the massive staircase leading to the second floor. When he finally deposits me onto his bed, I am already mush; a pool of want and need that only one person can satisfy. I reach for him, pulling him down on top of me.

Wanting no barriers between us, I rip at his clothing and my own; tearing at the fabric until every last piece has fallen away, leaving me bare beneath him.

Running his palm along my stomach, he sucks in a sharp inhale as his eyes travel across my bare torso, my chest, and then finally back to my face. His eyes are glazed, his arousal so clearly displayed that an instant burn comes to life inside of me; a feeling so intense that I feel like I may come apart below him even though he has barely touched me.

Climbing up my body, he settles in between my legs, his mouth finding mine instantly, peppering gentle kisses across my lips.

"Am I hurting you?" He whispers, kissing me again.

"No." I reassure him, knowing that he is being far gentler than he needs to be. "I'm tougher than I look." I give him a playful wink, pulling his mouth back down to mine.

He deepens the kiss, his tongue sweeping against mine as he slowly slides inside of me. The feeling of him as he inches deeper and deeper is incredible. This man knows how to make my body feel things I never knew possible.

Every touch is like fire, scarring my skin with the intensity of the burn. Every kiss is like being transported into another realm, one where we are the only two people in existence. Luke demands every part of me and I have no choice but to willingly give it to him.

His mouth never leaves mine as he slides slowly in and out of me, bringing both of our bodies to the brink and then rocking us back down again. He takes his time, making sure I feel every ounce of the pleasure he is fueling through my body.

I tug at his hair, scrape my nails down his sculpted

back, grip at his massive biceps as he forces my body higher and higher.

When he pulls back and meets my gaze, his crystal blue eyes burning into mine, I have no choice but to fall apart below him.

Luke holds my sight, refusing to let me look away as I ride out the pleasure surging through me.

He controls my body, forcing it to feel every ounce of him. He controls my mind, clouding everything around me until there is only him. And as I watch him give into his own pleasure, his eyes never leaving mine, I know he also controls my heart.

Mind, body, and soul… I am his.

Chapter Thirty-one

Samantha

How is it possible for me to find happiness knowing there is someone out there looking for me, someone prepared to kill me if, or rather when, they find me?

I know it sounds absurd. Absurd that just thirty-six hours ago I was running for my life and now here I am, snuggled up in the comfort of Luke's bed feeling like nothing and no one can touch me here.

Rolling to my side, I stretch my legs out while my arm immediately reaches for Luke. To my disappointment I find nothing more than a mess of blankets next to me. Peeling both eyes open, I blink rapidly into the bright sunlight pouring into the room.

Pushing up onto my elbows, I look around the empty space, letting my happiness really take hold before finally kicking the covers away. Swinging my legs over the side of the massive bed, the moment my feet hit the floor I spot a note on the bedside table, Luke's handwriting scrawled across the small piece of paper.

I had to head into the office for a little while. You looked so
peaceful I couldn't bear to wake you.
The alarm is armed so make sure not to
open any doors or windows.
Help yourself to anything in the house.
I'll be back as quickly as I can.
-Luke

I smile at his thoughtfulness, knowing that it probably took everything in him to leave me here alone. Pushing into a stand, I sit the note back where I found it before heading towards the bathroom. As much as I hate that Luke isn't here, I know he needs to maintain appearances for my sake.

He didn't make it to the office at all on Tuesday, not showing a second day would likely raise some red flags, especially where Ryan is concerned. Though I am not entirely convinced that Ryan would even suspect his brother considering he has no idea what has actually transpired between me and Luke over the last few weeks, especially our time in New York.

After showering and helping myself to a glass of orange juice and a banana, I decide it's time to start figuring out my next move. As much as I would love to just hide out here with Luke for the rest of my life, I know that is not a solution or even a real possibility.

It's been less than two days since I managed to escape Ryan. It's only a matter of time before it all catches back up with me and I need to be prepared when it does. Pushing open the French style doors to Luke's office, the moment I see his computer sitting on the large mahogany desk along the back wall, I start towards it.

Sliding into the high back leather chair, I open the laptop, relieved that it is not password protected. If I had to guess I would say this is the computer Luke has for recreational use and that there is nothing private stored on it.

Double clicking the web browser, I type *Sarah Trammell drug overdose* into the search engine and click on the first link the search populates. I am hoping that knowing what I know now will somehow help me find something I may have missed before. I know it's a long shot but at this point it's all I have to go on.

If I want any hope of taking Ryan down I need proof, so proof is exactly what I am going to try to find.

I am so lost in my research that when the door alarm chimes, I look up to find nearly three hours have passed. Unfortunately, I am no closer to finding anything that will help me.

My heart kicks up speed for a brief moment when the door alarm continues to chime for several seconds but then I hear the keypad beep and the alarm disable, letting me know it's Luke. Deciding I could use a break and maybe a second opinion, I push away from the desk and head out of the office.

Sliding my hand along the smooth rail, I make it about three quarters of the way down the slanted staircase before the main foyer comes into full view. The moment it does I freeze, fear paralyzing me on the spot.

"Well, well, well." Ryan crosses his arms in front of himself, his suit jacket pulling tightly against his broad shoulders as he does.

"Look at what I found." A pleased smile pulls up the corners of his mouth.

"Ryan." The name barely escapes my lips.

"Did you really think that I wouldn't find you?" His tone and demeanor is that of arrogance.

"I…" I start but the words stick in my throat and I can't seem to make them come out.

"You didn't call the police because you knew you couldn't prove anything." He continues without skipping a beat. "Choosing to keep who you are a secret over the few hours I may have spent in jail, while a ballsy move, will prove to be your fatal mistake." He tisks, slowly crossing the foyer towards the bottom of the staircase.

"You could have run, saved yourself. Instead you do nothing. You come to my brother and think that he's going to what; hide you away forever?" He lets out a humorous laugh like he's never heard something so funny before.

The sound echoes through the open space, bouncing off of the walls around me before dying off as quickly as it started. I hold his gaze, anticipating his next move. I know the moment the decision is made; I can feel the shift in the air and read the look in his eyes.

No more than seconds pass before I spin, knowing I need to run... Now!

"Where do you think you're going?" I hear the laughter in his voice just moments before his footsteps sound against the staircase behind me.

I know he's closing in on me, my speed no match for his. I can feel the fear mount with each second that passes but I refuse to turn around and look.

Five stairs from the top...

If I can just get to Luke's room, I can lock myself inside.

Four... My cellphone is on the nightstand.

Three... I can call for help.

Two... Almost there.

I feel a sudden tug on my left foot just as I reach the last step, the force pulling me off balance causing me to hit the landing on a hard thud. Pain shoots through my elbow, an involuntary cry sounding from my lips.

Within seconds I recover, attempting to get back up. I put my palms flat against the floor and try to push myself upwards but before I can make it even an inch I feel myself being pulled again, Ryan's grip on my left foot never wavering.

I hit the first two steps down hard, my hip cracking painfully against the edge of the marble as Ryan pulls me. Trying to kick at him with my right foot in an effort to free his grip on my left, my fight only seems to fuel his anger. He manages to snag my right foot just as it connects with his upper thigh, the impact having next to no effect on him.

Pulling at me violently, my head whips backwards from the force. The moment it connects with the stair behind me a vicious ring sounds through my ears. The second hit is even worse, causing black spots to blur my vision.

Trying to keep my head from hitting again, I twist

my body trying to take the impact of each step with my shoulder and hip rather than my back and head. This position proves harder to maintain with both of my legs restricted.

I manage to keep my head from hitting for at least a couple of steps before a twist in the staircase causes my body to hit at a different angle, the side of my face the next to connect to the hard surface below me.

I cry out from the impact, immediately feeling the blood flow down my cheek from just below my right eye. Ryan continues to drag me downward; the turn in the staircase making it hard for me to determine which part of my body will be take the brunt of the impact next.

Anticipating each step is almost as painful as the physical damage that follows. By the time we reach the large foyer below, I am convinced that not one part of my body made the trip down unharmed.

The moment I feel the flat surface beneath me I arch my back trying to give myself enough leverage to kick free but Ryan knows it's coming and is able to maintain his grip on me. I have the will to fight, the courage to stand up to him, unfortunately my small frame is no match for his large muscular one and he easily overpowers me.

"You're only making this harder on yourself." He says, his grip on my ankles so tight that I can literally feel the flow of blood to my feet being cut off, a tingling sensation spreading through my toes.

Twisting my legs, Ryan flips me to my stomach. I immediately try to pull myself up but I no more than get my weight up on my arms before Ryan gives my legs a violent tug and my body crashes to the hard floor below me.

"You want to know what I think is the saddest thing of this whole situation?" Ryan taunts, straddling my waist as he settles his weight down on my lower back, the pressure making it difficult to breathe normally.

"That you thought Luke would actually protect you." He laughs. "Did you really think he would choose you over his family?" He pulls my arms behind me, clearly planning to tie my hands together.

"He wouldn't do this to me." I spit, continuing to fight against Ryan's hold on me even though he barely budges.

"Oh but he did do this to you. How do you think I found out you were here?" I can see a large smile stretching across his face out of the corner of my eye.

"How do you think I got the security code for the alarm?" He continues. "Luke was just playing you Samantha. He was breaking down your guard. I'd say he did a pretty good job."

"Fuck you." I seethe, arching my back in an effort to push him off of me. "Luke would never do that." I scream, flailing violently beneath him.

"But he did." He lets out a spine chilling laugh, leaning forward so close that his lips graze my ear as he does.

The anger and desperation that floods through me over the thought that his words might just be true is overwhelming and before I even realize what I am doing the back of my head cracks loudly against Ryan's face, knocking him backwards.

His grip goes limp as the shock and pain shoots through him, the impact catching him enough off guard that I am able to use the momentum of the force to free my hands. I try to pull myself away using the strength of my arms, my legs still somewhat restrained under Ryan's weight, but he recovers too quickly for me to really get anywhere.

Ryan is easily able to reclaim his grip on me within seconds, securing both of my hands behind my back using only one of his.

"You really shouldn't have done that." He spits, his free hand wrapping tightly into my hair.

He lifts my head and then with one hard push cracks it against the marble floor, the impact causing the whole room to lose focus. I have no time to recover from the first blow before the second comes.

The pain radiates through my head, spreading down my neck and back, the darkness taking me under within seconds. Ryan's taunting laughter the last thing I hear before everything fades to black.

Chapter Thirty-two

Luke

The moment I realize the security alarm has been disabled, fear floods my body. Samantha didn't have the code so she would have set the alarm off had she tried to leave, which tells me everything I need to know...
She didn't go out, someone else came in.
"Sam." I immediately yell through the space.
"Sam." I repeat, louder this time.
Nothing...
I am met by a haunting silence, one that causes my pulse to thud so rapidly my own heart beat is the only sound in the room.
"Sam." I yell again, crossing the foyer towards the staircase, knowing if she's upstairs she may not be able to hear me.
Taking the stairs two at a time, the moment I reach the second floor I head directly towards the master bedroom. Spotting her cellphone lying on the bedside table, my mind instantly jumps to worst case scenario. Trying to shake off the thought, I search the other four bedrooms

before heading into the study, calling her name the entire time.

I know she's not here. I can feel it in my bones but I refuse to accept it. The moment I reach the top of the staircase I freeze. There's something there, something I can't believe I didn't see before.

Going down three stairs, I stop. Leaning down, I wipe my hand along the step, realizing the moment I look at the liquid on my fingers that it's blood. I nearly choke on my fear, panic making it impossible to react.

I follow the blood trail down, finding at least one spot on nearly every step. When I reach the bottom of the stairs, I scan my eyes along the foyer instantly spotting several more small droplets of blood starting from where I am standing and leading towards the back entrance.

Following the trail, it stops just a few feet from the private driveway that sits at the back of the house. Turning, I sprint back inside, knowing with almost complete certainty that Ryan must have found her but praying at the same time that I am wrong and that there is another reasonable explanation for this.

Pulling my cell from my jacket pocket, I punch in Travis' number and hit call, his voice sounding on the other end just as I push my way back inside the house.

"I need to know when the alarm system at the beach house was disabled this morning." I ramble, not bothering with pleasantries.

"Everything okay?" He asks curiously.

"Just tell me when the fucking code was entered." I demand.

"Give me a second." His response is immediate.

I can hear his hands working against the keyboard as he accesses the system.

"Eleven twenty-eight." He finally answers.

"Twenty minutes ago?" I ask in disbelief, realizing had I gotten here just a little earlier I could have prevented all of this.

"Looks like Nicholas's code was used to access the house." He adds.

"My father?" I question, realizing almost instantly that I when I changed my code to the house I never even considered changing his.

"I need you to track Ryan." I speak again before Travis can respond. "Find out where he is right now."

"It will take me a few minutes to pinpoint his location." Travis seems confused by my request but doesn't question it.

"Call me the moment you do." I end the call.

Pulling up my contacts, I press my father's name, impatiently waiting through ring after ring only to have his voicemail pick up. Disconnecting the call, I hit his name again. It only rings twice this time before his voices comes on the line.

"Luke, I'm in the middle of an important call." He immediately speaks.

"Were you at the beach house this morning?" I ask, ignoring his statement.

I know it's a long shot and that I am grasping but I need to make one hundred percent sure my father had nothing to do with this.

"Jack, I'm going to need to call you back." I hear my father speak, the call he's on clearly taking place from his office phone. "What it is Luke?" He sighs into the phone just moments later.

"Were you at the beach house this morning?" I

repeat, my tone reflecting my frustration.

"No, I've been at the office all morning, you know that." He adds, reminding me that I saw him shortly after I arrived at ScoTech this morning. "What's this about?"

"Ryan has her." I let the statement hang there as the realization hits me.

That's how Ryan got in. If he knew Sam was here then he also knew I would take extra precautions to keep her safe which would include changing the alarm code. And of course he knows Dad's code. How could I have been so careless?

I should have never left her.

"Ryan has who?" My father cuts into my thoughts, pulling me back to the conversation.

"Allie."

"Who?" My father asks, clearly not connecting the dots.

"Miss Reynolds." I clarify.

"Okay wait, what's going on?" His question only further fuels my anger and I try to keep my emotions in check.

"This is going to sound crazy." I say, not sure how exactly I am going to explain this to my father in the little time I can spare.

"Ryan attacked Miss Reynolds on Saturday and held her captive on the yacht for three days. She managed to escape a couple of days ago and has been hiding out at the beach house since then. This morning I had to come into the office to take care of a few things and when I returned, she was gone. There's blood on the floor and your alarm code was used to disable the alarm. I have Travis tracking Ryan's cell now but if you have any idea as to where he may have taken her you have to tell me now."

"Wait. Why would Ryan kidnap your assistant?" He

sounds genuinely confused.

"I don't have time to explain this any further but I promise I will explain everything later. Ryan will kill her if we don't find her in time." The thought is near crippling and I do my best to hold myself together.

"Let me see what I can do." He disconnects the call without another word. I no more than lock my phone before it springs to life in my hand again, Travis' name flashing across the screen.

"Did you find him?" I immediately answer.

"His phone is inside his office at ScoTech. We already confirmed with his secretary that it's there but he is not. She claims that she has not seen him all day so it's likely that he left it there overnight. We have no way to track his movements, no way of knowing where he is now."

"What about his car?"

"Still parked at the office." Travis says. "According to security footage of the garage he parked it there yesterday morning and it has not been moved since."

"So you're telling me he up and disappeared and we have no fucking clue how to find him?" I scream into the line, knowing this isn't Travis' fault but also not able to control the anger and fear bubbling inside of me.

"I'm sure he's fine." He tries to reassure me.

"This isn't about him. It's about the girl he abducted and is going to kill. Now find him!" I scream, ending the call before he can respond.

I can't stand the feeling of being so powerless. Samantha is out there right now, probably hurt and scared and there is not one damn thing I can do.

I'm terrified; terrified that I will never see her again.

Terrified that this is all my fault. I promised to keep her safe. She trusted me and I failed her.

If anything happens to her, I swear to God I'll never forgive myself.

Chapter Thirty-three

Samantha

I try to blink but my eyes feel like they have been glued shut, making it difficult to pry them open. I can hear humming. A near silent noise that barely makes it to my ears over the other sounds around me; footsteps, something that sounds like metal scratching against metal, and most prominently the rattle of chains which appear to be very close to me.

I feel pain… It's everywhere but mainly in my wrists. I feel like my hands are being pulled away from my body. A hard lump forms in my throat and I try to swallow it down only I can't because my mouth and throat feel too dry.

Finally managing to get my eyes open, I can see a concrete floor below me but it's hard to make out. Everything is blurred and hard to focus on, including the sight of my own feet as they lightly drag the surface of the floor, my toes barely able to reach it.

Managing to lift my head, the room starts to take shape around me. I'm in a warehouse, or something like a warehouse. The walls are rusted and peppered with small windows that appear to be painted black. I hear the chains again which prompts me to look up.

Only then do I realize that my wrists are handcuffed and linked through two large chains hanging above me. I immediately try to fight against the restraints but this only intensifies the pain further, the cuffs digging into my already wounded flesh so deeply it takes everything I have not to buckle from the pain.

"You won't get out of those on your own." Ryan's voice pulls my attention forward but rather than seeing him, I can only see a blurred image getting closer.

It isn't until he steps directly in front of me that I can finally make out his face.

"Pretty clever if you ask me." He draws my attention to the item in his hand as the metal scratching metal sound returns.

I take a shaky inhale when I realize where the sound is coming from; a hunting knife being run along a stone sharpener.

"What's wrong my dear Samantha, you seem nervous." He smiles causing my stomach to twist violently in fear.

"Please Ryan. Please don't do this. I swear I won't tell anyone anything. Please. Just let me go." My survival instinct starts to kick in and I know that if I don't try everything in my power to get out of this situation I am going to die very soon.

"But you already have, now haven't you?" He tisks, swinging the knife slowly in front of me. "You told Luke."

"But he's your brother." I try to reason with him. "You said so yourself, he would never choose me over his family." I repeat his previous statement back to him.

"He wouldn't. But that doesn't mean I'm going to

just let you go." He says, cocking his head to the side. "Now tell me, where should I start?" He smiles, holding the knife in front of me.

"Please Ryan." Emotion clogs my throat as he slides the back edge of the knife along my cheek and then down my jawbone.

"Please what?" He plays innocent. "Keep begging Samantha. I love to hear you beg." He flips the blade, slicing open the fabric of my shirt until it falls open in the center.

"I could have made you beg in so many ways but I'm sorry to say." He sets the tip of the blade against the edge of my collarbone. "That ship has since sailed." He whispers, sliding the knife downward.

I can feel the blade slice through my skin, the jagged edge ripping at my flesh as he trails it from the left side of my chest all the way to the bottom of my right side ribcage. I scream, the piercing sound bouncing off the walls back to me.

The pain is so unbearable that I slump my head forward, nearly losing consciousness. I can see the large gash running across my torso. I watch the blood as it flows down my body and hits the floor, each drop a sickening splash.

Ryan slowly circles me, the knife just inches from my skin as he does. I squeeze my eyes closed, waiting for the fatal blow to come but he's not done playing with me yet. Laying another long slash across my back, I can feel every ounce of pain as he slices me open shoulder blade to shoulder blade.

Once again my screams echo through the space, the

pain so agonizing it's disorienting.

"I suppose watching you die will be a lot like watching your brother die." Ryan says, watching the blood trickle down my back for several long seconds before stepping back in front of me.

Grabbing my chin, he forces my head up, making sure that I am listening.

"I remember watching him struggle to breathe. Watching him choke on his own blood and seeing the realization in his eyes that he was going to die. I want to see you look at me the same way." He sucks in a sharp inhale, a smile pulling up his mouth as he rears back and punches me directly in the stomach.

I swing backwards on the chains, the pain in my wrists blinding me from my inability to breathe, all the air forced from my body from the impact of the blow. I gasp and choke watching Ryan watch me, a look of complete satisfaction across his face.

When the chains finally come to a rest, Ryan lays a hard backhanded slap to my mouth, the impact splitting open my already injured lip, blood instantly pouring from the wound and flooding into my mouth.

"I'm going to watch you die and I am going to love every second of it." He holds the knife just below my belly button.

Before he can slice, I rear my head back and spit a mouthful of blood in his face, temporarily catching him off guard.

He stumbles backwards, frantically trying to wipe the liquid from his eyes. Pushing myself back as far as I can with only my tiptoes able to reach the ground, I swing forward and pull my feet up, laying a hit directly to his abdomen.

The contact knocks him off balance and he hits the

ground on a hard thud. Pushing myself back again, I am determined that if I die I will at least take a piece of him with me. The moment he stands I swing, once again pulling my feet up as I attempt to kick him again.

This time he expects it and catches my feet in the air, causing my wrists to support the entirety of my weight which proves nearly impossible to tolerate. I scream out, feeling like my hands are being torn completely away from my body.

Finally releasing me, Ryan allows me to swing backwards, making sure he is out of my reach until I am finally still again, my strength quickly fading the more blood I lose.

"I am going to cut you open piece by piece." He says, approaching me from behind. "I am going to bleed you dry." He reaches up, slicing my wrist open causing blood to pour down my arm.

I try to keep the pain inside. I try to hold it in and not let him have the satisfaction of my cries but when he slices the other wrist I can't contain it. It bursts out of me.

I can feel the blood now trailing down my other arm and I know what he's done. It will be only minutes now before I bleed out and then he will get exactly what he wants; to watch me take my last breath.

I feel the knife along my stomach but I am too weak to even hold my head up at this point. I am bleeding from four different areas and I can tell by the amount of blood pooling at my feet that I've already lost too much.

He puts pressure on the blade, the tip slicing into my flesh but then a man's voice suddenly floods the space and the blade falls away.

At first I think it's Ryan speaking to himself but then I realize that it's not Ryan at all, it's Nicholas, his father. The brief moment of hope I feel knowing another person is here quickly fades away when I realize that he is probably here to help his son clean up yet another mess.

I don't want to let my tears go but at this point my control over everything is slipping. They slide down my face, my last silent cry before I die at the hands of the very man who is responsible for killing every single person I have ever loved; every person with the exception of Luke.

His crystal blue eyes flash through my mind. Did he betray me? I refuse to believe it. I want to die believing that at least for a brief moment of time that I was loved and I was able to love in return.

The voices around me are muffled, my ears no longer able to distinguish specific sounds. They become louder until suddenly I realize there are no longer two men but several. I hear a loud crash followed by yelling but I can't focus.

I know I am seconds away from losing consciousness. I know that this is the end. I let my head go limp and I give up trying to support my weight with the tip of my toes. My whole body seethes with pain and I silently beg for death to take me.

I just want this to be over…

Just as the thought crosses my mind, I feel arms around me. The weight against my wrists vanishes and suddenly I feel like I am floating through the air. I feel the darkness pulling me under and I know this is the end.

But just when I feel it all slipping away, that's when I hear it… Luke's voice. It's faint at first but then grows stronger, demanding to be heard through the fog in my head.

I don't know if he's real or if he is simply a figment

of my imagination; a last glimpse of what I hold dearest just before it's over. Whatever it is I embrace it. I hold onto it. I follow it. Because wherever he goes, this world or another, that's where I want to be.

With that I let go and the world simply fades away...

Chapter Thirty-four

Luke

It's been seven hours since I arrived home to find Samantha gone. Seven grueling hours using every resource possible to find her and now that we think we finally have, I can't help but feel like it's too late. Too much time has passed. Too many things could have happened by now.

When I reach the strip of service warehouses my father purchased a few years ago there is already an ambulance and three police cars in the parking lot along with my fathers. Throwing my car into park, I kill the engine without even bothering to remove the keys.

Kicking the door open, I run towards the warehouse, terrified of what might be inside but even more terrified that we were wrong and that Samantha is not even here. The moment I push my way inside a police officer steps into my path.

"I'm sorry but you can't be in here." He says but his words barely register with me.

I am too busy scanning the room for Samantha to pay him any real attention. It takes only seconds for me to spot her. The moment I do I feel like someone has just punched me straight in the stomach, all the air leaving my body in an instant.

She is suspended in the air by her wrists, her feet barely brushing the ground as two officers work to remove her handcuffs and pull her down from the chains. There's blood everywhere. Her arms, her chest, her face, there isn't one inch of her that reflects the beautiful girl I left sleeping in my bed just hours ago.

The moment they get her free she collapses forward into their arms, her body so limp that I know right then and there that she must be dead. I can't handle the thought. Pain constricts my chest making it impossible to breath.

Turning, I spot Ryan just a few feet to my left, already restrained in handcuffs, two officers at his side. Without another thought I head towards him. My mind is blinded by anger; it's the only emotion I feel. I am too numb to process anything else.

Anger...

An officer tries to step in front of me just as I reach my brother but I shake him off. My fist connects with Ryan's face on a loud crack and he immediately goes backwards, hitting the ground with his hands cuffed behind him.

Before anyone can stop me I am on top of him. I draw back and hit him again, his nose splitting open from the impact. His blood makes me see her blood and only enrages me more until I no longer have control over my own body.

I unload, my fist connecting with his face at least two more times before one of the officers finally manages to pull me away. I look down over him feeling not one ounce of regret at what I see. His face is splattered with blood, his eyes already swelling.

"Calm down son." I hear my father's voice causing me to spin around, the officer that pulled me off of Ryan still holding onto my arm like he's unsure if it's safe to let me go.

My father approaches with two more police officers at his side. He stops just feet in front of me, nodding to the officer who is still trying to restrain me. I feel his hold immediately fall away as he takes a couple of steps back.

"Calm down." I scream, gesturing to where Samantha's body had been hanging moments ago. "He fucking killed her." The words stick in my throat.

"She's still alive." One of the officers cuts in, his words causing an entirely different feeling to flood through me.

"What?" I question, looking to where two of the officers are now escorting Ryan from the building.

"She's very badly injured and lost a lot of blood but she's still hanging on. They are taking her to the hospital now." The police officer standing closest to my father informs me.

Without a word I take off towards the door, spotting the ambulance the second I step outside. Running towards it, I scream Samantha's name.

"I'm here." I yell, the paramedic trying to get me to move so they can close the back door.

"Sir we need her to get to the hospital right away. She's lost a lot of blood. Please, I need you to step back."

"I'm here." I say again, doing as the paramedic asks.

He latches the door, not giving me even a glimpse of her before the lights flip on and the ambulance quickly pulls away.

"I'm sorry." I say to no one, the emotion so thick in

my voice that the words come out more of a sob than a real sentence.

Chapter Thirty-five

Samantha

I can hear faint noises in the background; a beeping noise that seems to go on forever.

Beep. Beep. Beep.

It's constant. It never stops.

I peel my eyes open, one and then the other, blinking rapidly through the brightness. It takes a few moments for my eyes to adjust as I look around the white sterile room trying to figure out where I am.

Ryan's face suddenly flashes through my mind and I sit up abruptly, pain shooting through my entire body as I do. The beeping noise increases and I look down to see various wires and I.V. tubes running up my left arm and across my chest.

I can feel myself starting to hyperventilate. It becomes harder and harder to breathe as flashes of images flip through my mind. Just when I feel like the panic will take me under, I hear something shuffle next to me which causes me to jump.

"Relax." I hear a voice next to me.

Flipping my eyes to the right, my breathing immediately accelerates when I realize there is a man sitting in the chair next to my bed. And that man is none other than Nicholas Scott.

"What are you doing here? What's going on?" I choke out, my throat raw and dry.

"Calm down. I'm not going to hurt you. Luke asked me to sit with you until he got back." He says, causing a mental image of Luke to flash through my mind.

"Luke." My voice comes out a half broken sob. "Where is he?"

"He's been here with you for the last two days. He has refused to leave your side but I finally convinced him to go get some coffee and fresh air. He should be back any minute."

"Ryan?" I choke out.

The reality that what I thought was a nightmare turning out to actually be the truth is a bit hard to swallow. It's clear based on the gauze wrapped up both of my arms and the soreness covering the rest of my body that it did really happen and somehow, someway, I survived; though the details of that survival are still foreign to me.

"In jail." Nicholas reassures me, standing from his seat. "Here, you need to lie back down or you're going to rip your stitches." He says, resting his hand gently on my shoulder and guiding me back down.

The bed is elevated so I am still propped up enough that I can see everything around me. Looking back to Nicholas, I have so many questions I don't even know where to begin. I open my mouth to say more but Nicholas speaks first.

"I know you probably have a lot of questions but right now all you really need to know is that Ryan cannot hurt you now. If it takes every penny I have, I promise you I will do everything in my power to ensure he never walks out of prison a free man." He rests his hand gently on top of mine.

"I can't make up for the hell my son put you through, and in large part I feel like I am partially responsible. I should have let him sit in jail after the car accident that killed your brother." He says, shocking me that he knows this information.

"I just thought he made a bad choice at the time and I didn't want his entire life to be ruined for that one decision. I know it doesn't make up for anything but one day when you have children of your own you will understand the need you have to protect them, sometimes even from themselves." He gives me a weak smile.

"Luke told me everything." He adds.

"I'm sorry I lied to you." I manage to get out.

I'm realizing that while I originally thought the entire Scott family was all one in the same, Ryan is really the only one that deserved my hatred. I feel suddenly guilty for ever tying Nicholas to anything. He's right, he was just trying to protect his child and can I really hate someone for that?

"Don't apologize." He shakes his head. "You had your reasons and I can respect that. I would probably have done the same thing if the tables were turned. Had I known the type of man Ryan had become, the type of man you knew he was, I never would have helped him all those years ago. I don't think any parent ever imagines their child would be capable of the things that Ryan did to you; the things he did to your brother and that poor girl." He shakes his head as if trying to shake the thought away, clearly devastated by Ryan's actions and learning the truth about his eldest son.

"I should probably let the doctors know you're awake." He gives me a weak smile.

"The police are also going to want a statement from you when you feel up to it." He adds, turning his attention to the door just as someone pushes their way inside.

The moment Luke's face comes into view, everything that has been bottled inside of me starts pouring out. Tears flood my vision as he rushes to my side, his hand sliding gently down the side of my face.

"I'm so glad you're okay." He whispers, breaking eye contact for a short second to nod at his father who immediately turns and leaves the room.

"What happened?" I ask Luke, swiping at a tear that breaks free down my cheek.

"Ryan had you in an old warehouse that my father owns. We looked for you for hours but it was my father who actually found you. If it wasn't for him…" He fades out, the thought clearly too much for him to bear.

"I thought I lost you." He says, sliding onto the edge of my bed, turning inward to face me. Taking my hand gently in his, he works slow circles across the back with the pad of his thumb.

"Hey." I whisper, pulling his gaze back to me. "You didn't." I reassure him. "Because of you I am alive." I pause. "He tried to convince me that you betrayed me, that you told him where I was." His eyes widen at my words.

"Samantha you know me…" I hold my hand up to his lips, silencing him.

"I know. I know you would never do that to me." I reassure him, letting my hand fall away.

"I'm so sorry. I promised to protect you." I can tell

he absolutely blames himself for this.

"This isn't your fault. I came here knowing the risks. I put myself in this situation. I am the one that chose not to call the police. I am the one that was so hell bent on my own revenge that I couldn't see what I would be losing. I am the *only* one responsible for what happened to me. You don't get to carry that with you. You saved me. You gave me a reason to fight." I reach up, running my fingers along his scruffy jaw.

He hasn't shaved for at least a handful of days and I must say, the look suits him.

"I like this." I scratch at the hair, seeing the seriousness fade from his expression and the lighthearted man I know come to life.

"Oh yeah?" He gives me a heart melting smile.

"Yeah." I smile, pulling his face down to mine.

He lays the softest kiss against my lips before pulling back and meeting my gaze.

"I love you." His words barely come out a whisper, my chest constricting the moment they reach my ears. "I think I've known it since New York." He fades out for a moment, lost to his thoughts.

"I watched you sleep for nearly two days." He finally continues. "And all I could think was what I would do if I never got the chance to tell you how much you mean to me." His words cause my heart monitor to spike in speed, the beeping coming increasingly faster across the machine.

"I know it's fast and so much has happened but I just needed you to know. I needed to at least say it once. I…" I cut off whatever he's about to say.

"I love you, too." I blurt out, his eyes widening the moment the words leave my lips. "I love you." I say more clearly, watching the elation that takes over his handsome face.

I never dreamed I would say these words to another living soul again. I didn't think I was capable of feeling the way Luke makes me feel. He makes everything okay.

He doesn't erase what's happened to me, no one can change the events that mold who we become. But he makes the past bearable. He makes the future possible. He makes me dream of what life can be.

Giving me an incredible smile, he drops another gentle kiss to my mouth before resting his forehead against mine.

"It's you and me now." He whispers.

"You and me." I agree.

Epilogue

Samantha

Two Years Later…

I slide the brush along the canvas allowing the tip to glide freely across the surface. A warm breeze comes in from the ocean, pulling my attention back to the waves that crash onto the beach below me.

Taking a deep breath of fresh sea air, I turn my focus back to the canvas, jumping slightly when a pair of arms slide around me from behind, settling on my swollen stomach.

"How are my two favorite people today?" Luke's voice washes over me just moments before he drops a kiss to the crook of my neck.

"Your son could take it a little easier on his mama." I laugh, snuggling into his embrace.

Swiping the brush one more time, I drop it into the water before turning in Luke's arms. The moment my husband's handsome face comes into view I can't help but smile.

"Good morning." I breathe, pushing up on my tip toes to place a light kiss to his lips.

"Good morning." He smiles, placing his hands on

my stomach.

Leaning down he drops a kiss to the top of my belly before speaking directly to it.

"Now, Sean Nicholas, I need you take it easy on your mom kiddo." He fakes seriousness, before straightening his posture and pulling me to him, wrapping his arms around my shoulders.

"There, problem solved." He laughs, kissing the top of my head.

"Oh I'm sure he's gonna listen to that." I giggle, burying my face into his chest as I inhale his incredible scent.

"I like what you're working on." He says, prompting me to turn my head towards the painting.

"I think I'm going to put it in the nursery." I smile, letting my eyes travel along the splashes of blues and greens.

"I think that sounds perfect." He turns my face back towards him, his lips immediately finding mine.

"I love you Mrs. Scott." He rubs his nose gently against mine.

"I love you too, Mr. Scott." I smile. "Now stop distracting me." I shove at him playfully, shooing him off of the balcony.

"Yes dear." He laughs, disappearing back inside.

Turning back towards the canvas, it's clear to see the painting represents exactly how I am feeling in this moment as most of my art does; at peace.

It's funny how life works out.

When I arrived in Los Angeles two years ago I had one goal in mind. I never expected to have a life beyond my revenge. And while Ryan has paid, and continues to pay from a prison cell, it's not his outcome that gives me peace, it's my own.

I thought the day Ryan was sentenced it would all be over, like somehow it would all magically just be okay. And while the judge sentenced him to twenty-five years to life for my kidnapping and attempted murder, at the end of the day it didn't give me much peace.

Don't get me wrong, I'm glad Ryan is finally where he deserves to be. But I finally realized that the words my mother said to me all those years ago actually rang true. There really is no peace in vengeance. We must learn to forgive and through that forgiveness will find the means to let go.

So that's what I have done; forgiven. It didn't happen overnight but eventually as months passed, I finally learned to let go; of the pain, the heartache, the regret.

Little by little I found peace.

Because at the end of the day I finally realized one very important thing…

Ryan may have destroyed my past, but he also gave me back my future.

MELISSA TOPPEN

The End

Beyond Love Lies Deceit Playlist

I draw so much inspiration from music and I would like to extend a huge THANK YOU to every single one of these artists for their amazing gift of music.

Before I Sleep- Joy Williams
Until We Go Down- Ruelle
Even Though I Say- Saint Asonia
Fight Song- Rachel Platten
Terrible Love- Birdy
Til it Happens to You- Lady Gaga
Alive- Sia
Deep End- Ruelle
Circles- Jana Kramer
Revival- Selena Gomez
I Was Me- Imagine Dragons
Wildfire- Demi Lovato
You Matter to Me- Sara Bareilles Feat. Jason Mraz
Can You Hold Me- NF

BEYOND LOVE LIES DECEIT

MELISSA TOPPEN

Made in the USA
Columbia, SC
05 October 2022